The Thugtress of Harlem 2

-Nadir

The Thugtress of Harlem 2

Word to Vince Presents

Mailing List

Click link below and join my mailing list to stay up to date with new releases, sneak peeks, giveaways, and much more…

https://bit.ly/48m7Sm9

Table of Contents

Chapter 1

Big Bear felt like a million bucks as he stepped out the courtroom. Given a full reversal on his case, he was a free man now. He could not stop smiling.

Thank you, God!

Spending nearly six years behind bars, a heavy burden had been lifted off his shoulders when the judge made his final decision on record.

"Mr. DuPont here was clearly not responsible for the crime he stood convicted of and deserves to be home with his family, also compensated for the time he spent away from his loved ones," the judge ruled.

Big Bear was an actual participant in the murder he stood convicted of but had gotten away with the crime, *scott free.* He was framed, though, by corrupted police officers, and sent to rot in prison.

The victim was a worker for the DuPont's who decided to steal from the family. Learning of the man's thievery, Big Bear lured him to a vacant street and put a bullet in the center of his head. Out of eye and ear shot of anyone. Somehow the police caught wind of his involvement in the murder, brought him in for questioning, and eventually charged him for the crime. He denied involvement in the murder but was accused of writing a sworn statement implicating himself in the crime. This fictious statement, signed by a rogue officer using his signature, was the chief reason for his eventual 25-to-Life sentence.

However, foul play by the police eventually came to light and he was given a reversal.

Thank the lord!

"Mr. DuPont," called the judge, "have a nice life," was his final words.

Big Bear did not need to hear anymore. He walked out the courtroom in a hurry, even as his attorney called to him.

"One second, Mr. Dupont," the attorney called.

But Big Bear kept it moving. If the lawyer wanted to talk, they could talk outside of the courtroom where he would have more of a chance to get away if the judge so happened to change his mind. Returning to prison was not an option. He would rather die. *Fuck that.* The years he spent behind the wall was a reminder that he'd better cherish his freedom. *Maybe* slow down a bit this time around. Especially now that he got a reversal.

"Congratulations, Mr. DuPont," applauded his attorney once outside the courtroom.

"Yeah, yeah, whatever man," said Big Bear, brushing the man off.

He went over to his wife, Cheryl, who was present throughout the entire proceedings and now stood outside the courtroom.

"What's up, babe?" he greeted with a huge smile.

Opening her arms for an embrace, Cheryl waited to feel the love of her life, *Big Bear.* When he got within her grasped, he held onto to her like he never had before. It felt so good to feel her man after so many years. She really missed her Big Bear, a nickname she gave him years ago.

"Welcome home, baby."

"Damn, I missed your scent," said Big Bear, sinking his nose deep into Cheryl's neck, sniffling aloud like a dog. Being able to hold his wife was a dream come true. He'd dreamt about this day for years. It finally came to reality.

"I missed yours, also, baby."

Releasing his grip on Cheryl, Big Bear turned to his attorney.

He said, "I'll be by to see you tomorrow. Family time now."

"I understand, Mr. DuPont. I'll be at the office when you're ready."

Big Bear turned to Cheryl.

"Let's go," he instructed.

Outside the courthouse, a chauffeured stretch Mercedes limousine, guarded by two bodyguards, awaited Big Bear and Cheryl.

Big Bear greeted the hulky men, family workers, before getting inside with Cheryl. Resting back in the comfy leather seats, he cracked a smile at his wife.

"I still can't believe this shit. I was just in jail this morning, now I'm in a limousine," he said, still in shock by how things played out in his case.

As Big Bear, Cheryl rested back in her seat.

"You better believe *this shit*. It's real. You're free like a bird," she said.

Cheryl was right. He was free. He didn't have to pinch himself to awaken from a dream. The powers that be had opened the cells of the penitentiary letting him out, a chance many had not received. He was blessed. The God up above granted him the opportunity to get back to business. And that he would do. *Get back to business.*

"You're right, babe. It's work time," he said. "Driver," he called to the chauffeur.

"Yes, Mr. DuPont."

"Take us to the fanciest restaurant Manhattan has to offer."

"No problem. I know just the spot."

Pulling up to Mr. Chows in Manhattan's Tribeca neighborhood, Big Bear and Cheryl was let out the ride and ushered inside the trendy restaurant. The fancy joint was filled with whites, A-list celebrities, musicians, sports stars. All dining on expensive dishes.

Searching the room, Big Bear penetrated everyone. He was glad to be present inside one of the best restaurants instead of a prison cafeteria. Directed to a table, someone called to him as he strolled through the luxurious atmosphere. He stopped to see the caller.

It was a Harlem rapper who had become a superstar during his time away. He'd funded the man's career at the beginning of his rise to fame.

"That's you, Sport," smiled Big Bear.

The rapper, known as Sport, got up to greet Big Bear, bowing before the man as if he were a king.

"Yeah, b. It's me," he said. "And you know I owe you a lot. I'm *really* glad to see you made it home."

"Thanks."

Giving Sport a few minutes of his time, he exchanged information with the rapper before going over to sit with Cheryl.

"That's Sport from '38th Street," he said.

"I know. He used to stop by to see Kevin all the time," Cheryl replied.

Hearing Kevin's name dampened Big Bear's mood. Cheryl, who had carried him for nine months, must have felt the same way. He still didn't believe his son was gone. It *still* hurt every time he thought about Kevin. *He should have still been around to hold down the family*, thought Big Bear. He should have been there to see him released. But he wasn't, and it hurt. Catching himself before he got emotional, he changed course in the conversation.

"How's Drac doing? You heard from him?"

"Yeah. He should be calling me later. He usually calls during the night hours."

"He's holding up good?"

"You know that son of ours is a warrior. Just like his daddy."

"He better be. No punks allowed in this family."

"Trust me. He's one boy you don't have to worry about."

"What am I hearing about this so-called wife of his. When did he get married?"

Word got to Big Bear that Drac put his wife in position to run the family, a blasphemous act, one he didn't agree with one bit. When he got this information, he wished he had the opportunity to speak to Drac to give him a piece of his mind. The girl, Lady, as he was told she was named, was making raves in the streets in the name of the DuPont's. He didn't like this. Especially when he heard she and Mark, his nephew, was at war. This shouldn't have been able to occur.

"She's a good girl," Cheryl spoke up for Lady. "I really like her. And she has Drac's best interest at heart."

"But she's a *bitch*, and a *bitch* can't control the family. You know that."

Especially not an outside bitch.

This Lady should not have been allowed to get involved in family business. Regardless of Mark's antics, she was not to intervene with what the DuPont's had going on.

"When you meet her, I think you'll think different about her," said Cheryl, brushing off Big Bear.

She knew her husband like the back of her hand. So it was no surprise that he disagreed with Lady leading the family. He had no idea of how great a woman Lady was though. The back-and-forth with Mark rocked Harlem, leaving many on their tippy toes. Lady led an army from Polo Grounds that was laying it down, gunning down Mark's troops whenever they got the chance. *As they should.* Cheryl didn't like how Mark was acting out and wanted him dead. He killed Fred, Bull, and Spank, all men she had good relationships with. His greed drove him to get rid of some great men, and he needed to be disciplined for his foul actions.

"I don't really wanna know her. I'm home now, so I'll bring back the family as one."

Home now, Big Bear was sure his presence would tame the raging fire in Harlem. Afterall, he was the king of Harlem, the lord over *all* lords.

Cheryl left things how they were. Debating with Big Bear would prove nothing. He had always been an arrogant, *sure man*, who ignored opinions of others. Trying to explain Lady's loyalty, business etiquette, and leadership skills would fall on deaf ears. Big Bear wouldn't care about any of that. It was his way or the highway. Had always been that way.

"Let's get in our order," she said.

"Yeah, let's do that."

Chapter 2

The DuPont battle was the trending topic in the city. Daily, deadly gunbattles marred the streets of Harlem and the Bronx, back-and-forth bouts between Lady and Mark's men. The world wind of violence seemed like it would never end.

The cat was out the hat. Mark now knew Lady was controlling the family on Drac's side of things and was gunning for her.

On the other hand, Lady long had a target on Mark's head, waiting for the day he slipped up so she could send a missile through his face. She was anxious to rid the world of the thorn in Harlem, Mark. His disloyalty toward the family made her hate his guts. He deserved a dirt nap, somewhere he would never be found ever again.

Being a part of the DuPont world taught Lady about investments. The amount of property and businesses the family owned was unbelievable. Hotel chains; farms; clubs; houses; food chain franchises. The list went on-and-on. Big Bear was surely a billionaire, Drac a millionaire. Neither had to participate in street activities. Nevertheless, that's what they chose, and she was along for the ride. *For the time being at least.*

Polo Grounds was flaming hot, so Lady kept a low profile in Queens, pressing buttons from the circumference of her home. She moved her mother out the projects, *literally* forcing her to come and stay out in Queens.

"I don't want to leave," argued her mother, defiant about the move.

"Well, you're gonna have to, or end up with a bullet in the head," Lady warned.

This scared her mother. Lady revealed her newfound position, elaborating on the serious enemy forces hunting her.

"They won't stop at nothing to get to me, even it means kidnapping you to use as bait. So you better pack your shit and let's go."

Shooter Sean checked in every day, keeping her abreast with what was going on in the neighborhood, daily operations.

It was something new every day. In the past week, two Young Gunners were killed, shot to death by Jamaican gunmen while standing on W. 155th.

"Shit is hotter than it's ever been out here," mentioned Shooter Sean.

Lady responded, "And it's only gonna get hotter."

Mark no longer kept his connection to the Jamaicans a secret. His plan of taking over the family was more evident now than ever before. This had always been his mission, but at first, he was trying to not be so blatant with his maneuvers. He first sent in the Jamaicans to Polo Grounds knowing Kevin wouldn't accept their presence and would more than likely take on the political marksmen and be killed during the process. Though the Jamaicans were successful with killing Kevin, Mark didn't know it would drag on for so long after the murder, revealing his deceit during the process. He figured they would eventually kill Kevin and that would be it. But Drac got involved, Jamie revealed his ties to the Jamaicans, and everything spiraled out of control. Mark was placed on the spot. Put in the hot seat. *Exposed.*

Instead of submitting to his death, though, he decided to fight it out for control of the family.

Preparing to go and see Drac, a phone rang in the background. Her mother answered, bringing the device to her.

"Some rude man wants to speak to you."

Lady took the phone from her mother.

"Hello," she said.

"Listen, I'm a get right to the point. Whatever you had going on, it's over now. This Big Bear."

"Big Bear?"

Lady looked at her mother, wide-eyed. She was surprised her mother didn't recognize the man's voice, seeing that the two were once an item. Clearly, Big Bear didn't recognize her mother's voice either.

"Yeah. Big Bear. I'm back around, so you can fall back."

Drac informed Lady that Big Bear had gotten a reversal on his case and would be released soon, but she didn't believe it would be *so* soon. The man's aggressive tone threw her for the loop; she was surprised to hear from him.

"Okay," was all she could think to say.

How could she argue with Big Bear? He was *the* head DuPont, *over even Drac*, and had to be respected as such. Though she had a personal vengeance for Mark, who played a key role in Jamie being murdered, she had no choice but to fall back.

Big Bear was home and had spoken.

Big Bear hung up in her ear.

"Big Bear is home," she said to her mother right away.

"I'm surprised I didn't recognize his voice," said her mother.

"Me, too."

Gathering her things, Lady hit the road to go and see Drac.

Making it to the jail in about an hour, she went through the usual process of being thoroughly searched before being let onto the visit floor. Once through with the process, she entered a noisy, packed room with family and friends who'd come to see jailers. Directed to a seat, she sat and waited on Drac.

Monitoring the room, her eyes came upon a man who ice grilled her. Quickly returning the gesture, she cracked a smirk before turning away. She was not going to be eye fighting with a nigga.

Fuck is his problem?

Drac eventually came down.

"Who's that nigga?" Lady asked right away, gesturing at the man who was watching her.

Stealing a glimpse at the man, Drac recognized him right away. It was one of Mark's soldiers who'd recently came to the jail. He had an eye fight with the man just the day before in the jail's cafeteria.

"That's one a Mark's niggas."

"Before you came down, that nigga was screwing me. I was wondering where the fuck he knows me from to be looking at me that way."

Drac could tell Lady didn't know she was making raves in the underworld of Harlem. Word had gotten back to him about missions she'd sent soldiers out on, daring ones that produced notable casualties. One of Mark's top lieutenants, a Spanish man from the Bronx, became a victim to Lady's wrath when she sent some Young Gunners to his house after finding out where he lived. Twenty shots later, he was all over the news. *Dead.* This was a big win for the team, a victory Drac praised Lady for. Her reputation was growing by the day, sounding off even in the cellblocks of jails.

"I don't think you know how popular you're becoming." He smiled.

"But I don't want to be popular, babe," said Lady, giving Drac the puppy dog face. "I try to stay as low as possible, under the radar."

"This is the life of a boss, babe. You gotta roll with the punches. It's just how it is."

Lady didn't like that her name was getting out there. This put her in more danger than she was already in. Fighting a battle against seasoned vets as Mark wasn't an easy job. Had she not had the heart to stand up to him, she would have been left New York as a whole.

"I just hope my name isn't in the police mouth like they're in everybody else's."

"I hope so, too."

"Anyway, just keep an eye on that nigga over there." Lady made a covert gesture to Mark's soldier. "That nigga look mad about something."

"That nigga better play his position before he ends up with a piece of metal through his face."

Lady smiled, knowing that Drac meant every word he said. There was no doubt in her mind that Drac would kill the man if he got the chance. However, she hoped it didn't reach such a level. He was already fighting two jail cases and two bodies. He didn't need any extras on his plate.

"On another note, I got a call from your father. He's back out, and ain't playing any games," she said.

"Word?"

Drac's mother told him, the night before, that Big Bear was released but he didn't get the chance to speak with his father yet.

He asked, "What he say to you?" He thought about asking how Big Bear got her number but remembered who his father was. Big Bear could get anyone's number, *anytime.*

That's how powerful he was.

Lady explained the exchange with Big Bear.

"So," she shrugged her shoulders, "I guess I'm back on the sidelines."

The disrespectful way in which Big Bear dealt with Lady angered Drac, but there wasn't much he could really do about it. His father would always be who he was. *An arrogant, bad motherfucker.* It was no surprise about the way he spoke to Lady. So even though it was upsetting, Drac just had to accept it.

"It's a whole new ballgame out there now, babe. And I don't think my father knows that," he said. "All his past shooters are now at the age where they're just chilling and raising their families. He's pretty much naked without *us* as the youngsters."

Lady shook her head. Drac was right.

"You're one hundred percent right. But your father has to figure that out himself," said Lady, accepting the fact that she had no power to speak out against Big Bear.

"Just keep the troops in place. I'll speak to him probably later on."

"Okay."

Chapter 3

Mark felt like a punk.

A bitch ass nigga!

How come he had not gotten rid of the bitch from Polo Grounds *yet*, he thought to himself every day.

The young bitch at that.

With his street experience, it should have been an easy job to wipe her off the face of the planet. But for some peculiar reason, he could not get a line on her. Everybody he sent her way came back either with bullet wounds or in a body bag. He'd never witnessed a set of boys from Polo Grounds get down as the current flock in control of the projects. Not even Kevin's team moved so hard. *Nor Big Bear's.*

Drac equipped his wife with a gang of snipers who were willing to die for their queen.

He had to admit, Drac was smart. Marrying the girl, who Mark had come to find out was named Lady, was a power move. Through her, Drac had all rights to continue his hold on the family, even while he was away in jail.

Mark would have never thought Drac would make such a chess move. But he did, and now it was costing Mark his men. His business. And possibly his freedom. The police were down his neck, watching him like a hawk. Because of the war, the heat was on. He barely could walk with his gun. Most of the time he made a move outside, he was pulled over by the cops. His car, almost every time, was searched for something to stick and send him away.

"I'm gonna catch you motherfucker," threatened one cop during a stop. "Even if it costs me my job."

The officer was from the 46th Precinct in the Bronx who'd been patrolling 183rd for years, hounding Mark's regime. Mark knew to stay clear of the man, *always had*, but the current war heightened crime in the neighborhood, giving the police more work to do. Which they were angry about. So much that they were willing to set him up if need be. Thus, he was forced to keep a low profile, far away from his block.

Lying low in Brooklyn, he only came out when he had to, that being to handle some business for the family, or to maybe catch a bite with some pretty-young-thing he met and was courting to dick-down. Other than that, he stayed indoors. Donovan stopped by to check on him every so often. The man's soldiers were a significant part of the war, fighting the Young Gunners daily in Harlem. One thing about Donovan's crew, they were outliving Mark's faction. The Jamaicans were nothing to play with, one of the reasons why Mark connected with them.

"Shit is going crazy out in Harlem and the Bronx," said Mark to Donovan, who'd stopped by to check on him. "Those little motherfuckers are driving way from Harlem to the Bronx to kill my guys. We gotta catch that little nigga, Shooter Sean."

"That's what I wanted to speak to you about," said Donovan, also agitated by the way things were going with the war.

He thought his men would have long brought a calm to things by killing off the Americans, but that was not the case. The Americans were fighting a tough fight, not backing down for anything.

"What's up? Don't tell me it's more bad news, man."

Mark didn't want to hear any more bad news. Of late, that's all he'd been hearing.

"No. This is good news. I found out where the bitch mother's boyfriend stays. One of my soldiers knows her mother really well. She's a drunk."

"Does she go by the boyfriend's house?"

"All the time. So we can kidnap her and use her as bait."

This was great news. Mark felt like jumping for joy. If he couldn't get to Lady, grabbing her mother, *and killing the old bitch*, would make him happy.

He said, "Let's go stake out the place now."

"I already got two niggas doing that."

Rubbing his palms together, Mark smiled a huge smile. Taking out a phone to make a call, someone so happened to call him.

He answered, "Who this?"

"Who this?" the caller asked. "This Big motherfucking Bear, nigga!"

It had been years since Mark heard his uncle's voice but knew right away it was Big Bear. *How the fuck he get my number,* he wanted to ask, but refrained.

"What's going on, Unc'?" he asked, keeping his cool.

"I need to see you now! Where you at? I'm pulling up on you."

Mark looked over at Donovan who returned a confused look. He did not know yet who Mark was speaking to on the phone.

"Come on, man, Unc,' you're joking right?"

Mark wanted to ask Big Bear *how the fuck could you pull up on me when you're in prison?*

"Do I sound like I'm joking? I'm in Harlem now. Where could we meet up at?"

Big Bear sounded serious. Mark's heart began to race. Was his uncle really home? Or was this a set up to get him to a certain place for Drac to send men to kill him?

"I'm not around right now. I'm outta town," he lied.

If Big Bear was actually home, there was no way he would meet up with the man, anyhow. At the end of the day, Big Bear was Drac's father, and he knew the man wouldn't put his nephew before his son.

"When you getting back in town?"

"I should be back by the weekend."

"Make sure you report to me as soon as you get back."

Big Bear hung up the phone before giving Mark the chance to respond.

Shocked, Mark held the phone in the air, looking from Donovan to the device then back at Donovan.

Big Bear's finally home, he thought. *But how?*

The last he heard, Big Bear had a 25 to Life sentence and had only been down about five to six years. Therefore, he had at least twenty more years before he was eligible to see a parole board, who could hit him for the rest of his life. Which would be the case in his case. Big Bear was a brutal guy. A terror who intimidated the streets of Harlem for years. No parole board would want him back on the streets. Was he really home?

Mark had to get to the bottom of this.

"What happened?" Donovan asked, seeing how Mark was acting weird.

Finally catching himself, Mark explained the phone conversation to Donovan.

"What?"

Donovan was taken aback by the news.

Mark shook his head.

"You know we're gonna have to kill him?" Donovan asked.

Big Bear would have to be killed, *without a question*. After all that had taken place, there was no way Big Bear would allow Mark to get away with what occurred. And, as far as taking over the family, that was out the window. Especially now that Big Bear was home. Everyone would naturally side with the true boss, *Big Bear*.

"Things are gonna get real ugly now," he said out loud.

Donovan sucked his teeth.

"That's a easy kill. We'll get to Big Bear. But let's focus on kidnapping this bitch mother. She did too much, and deserves a dirt nap," he said.

"You're right. Let's set it up," said Mark.

If Big Bear was really home, *it is what it is*. The streets had changed since Big Bear was running around years before; the older general had better know what he was doing. If he slipped up, he could catch a bullet. Mark would not hesitate to send him to hell if need be. He did not fear his uncle. He did respect what he did in the past. But someone's street reputation was as good as their last act of violence. One had to keep proving themselves in the concrete jungle of New York City. Thus, Big Bear would have to prove, *again*, if he was really built like that. During the course of him doing so, Mark would be on his heels with his Jamaican and Bronx posse's.

Chapter 4

Big Bear spent most of the day reorganizing things throughout Harlem. Going from block to block, he let everyone know he was back. Checking in on some of his businesses, he met up with managers of the establishments and collected cash. One thing he could give his sons, they kept things in order when it came to his businesses. Everything seemed to be on point. He was proud of his boys, even Kevin, who was no longer around in the physical form. They made sure he was straight, even while he was away.

Something he did notice, though, when checking in on his many businesses, he learned that Mark had been stopping by to lay pressure down on his workers and business partners. He extorted money from the establishments, claiming to be the new leader of the DuPont's.

This infuriated Big Bear.

It would be a matter of time before he killed Mark. Drac had warned him about the man, but he failed to take heed, sticking to principles of the past. He'd set up a system within the family that he stressed to be implemented. *DuPont's are not to go against DuPont's.* A golden rule that, obviously, Mark held no regard for. Who was he to disregard what was created before he was able to come out the house?

The little nigga gotta die!

Returning to Polo Grounds at night, Big Bear took a seat on a bench outside, alone. The place seemed deserted. Obviously, no one wanted to be caught by one of Mark's henchmen, who he learned had been consistently circling the projects to catch off-point stragglers. Also, the Jamaicans were a constant nag, coming through spraying shit up, *recklessly*, not caring who they hit.

Big Bear understood that his people did not wanna get caught slipping. Drac's crew, the Young Gunners, were doing a great job fighting back, but the pressure was on. With all he'd been through in the past, in the streets, no war he fought ever reached the extent of the current war in effect. Usually, he crushed his enemies quick and fast. The current bout, however, didn't seem like it would end anytime soon. Too much blood had been spilled. Too many bodies had dropped.

He surely missed home.

Polo Grounds.

Though he was born on the eastside of Harlem, his family moved west when the Polo Grounds Towers was first built in 1968. His mother got one of the first apartments through a welfare program, a pad he held dear to heart and still had a key to. It was a pad in the Bear Cave that he turned into a drug den after his mother passed on and he got involved in the game.

Poverty was a reality during his come up. His family was dirt poor, unable to fend for themselves. There were many hungry nights at home with no food. He watched his mother struggle with three jobs to try and feed him and his siblings, *even that wasn't enough*. When he turned twelve, he decided enough was enough. He had to do something about his situation. Something to help his family.

Men from all over Harlem saw Polo Grounds as an open drug market and began to set up shop in the projects. Drug addicts were everywhere. The place resembled a zombie town. This was during the heroin era of the '70s and everyone was strung out on the drug. Addicts crowded the projects, nodding off in building hallways with needles stuck in their veins. Big Bear had even dibbled-and-dabbled in using the drug but quickly regained his senses. Instead, he figured out a way to make money off heroin. He found out early in life that hustling wasn't his forte, well, at the time, so he became a stick-up kid.

He was a big kid, bulky in figure. Some thought he was much older than his age during his come up in the seventies, but, at the time, he was in his late teens pushing twenty. Growing up, he and his brothers fought like cats-and-dogs, so he knew how to throw down. He became super nice with his hands. He beat up most kids his age, and even older, in the projects, garnering himself a reputation that resounded even outside the projects. His powerful punches cracked jaws and laid niggas out in Harlem. He was a force to be reckoned with.

Running down on hustlers, he would strongarm the men right before stripping them of their belongings. He became infatuated with being the big dog in the projects and wanted all the hustlers, especially the ones who were not really from Polo Grounds, to know that he was not to be played with.

Eventually he got a grip on Polo Grounds, bringing his brothers along on the takeover. Together, they robbed local hustlers. Those they had a little bit of sympathy for, they allowed to pay a weekly tax. People began to call them the DuPont brothers, birthing what Big Bear would head as a billion-dollar empire.

Once Big Bear got a foot hold in Polo Grounds, he began to branch out to other sections of Harlem. This was when he experienced the wrath of some tough figures, who challenged his bully ways.

Spank, who eventually became his good friend, was one of the men who was not having it.

Big Bear would frequent 139th, which eventually became one of his main domains, and bully the guys on the block. Though the pack from 139th was a tough set, they were unable to withstand the pressure of Big Bear. By then he was playing with guns and had morphed into a real-life killer. His animalistic behavior scared many on 139th. *But not Spank.*

Spank challenged Big Bear, *every time*, taking him on in gun-battles, shooting it out whenever they saw one another. They were constantly at each other's neck, neither party backing down. During one of their battles, Big Bear's gun ran out of bullets and Spank got right up on him, gun in hand. Accepting defeat, Big Bear waited on Spank to take his life, but the strangest thing happened. Spank, instead of sending him home to his maker, put out a hand for a shake.

"We don't need to be fighting. We need to be on the same team," said Spank.

Big Bear could not believe what was taking place. If he caught Spank in the same position, he would have surely ended the man's life. But Spank gave him a pass. One that he held dear to heart and created a lifelong bond for. He and Spank became the best of friends; together they took over many blocks in Harlem.

Spank played a key role in expanding the DuPont family.

When he was established in Harlem as a dominant force, Big Bear called a meeting with his family. Meeting up, he laid down rules.

"The DuPont's are one. A DuPont can't kill another DuPont. DuPont's do not fight against one another. Every dollar a DuPont brings in must be shared with the family. Only a DuPont could run the family, no one else," Big Bear voiced rules he created.

As time went on, he established more rules, the core of which were mentioned at that first meeting. Soon, the DuPont's became huge. Money began to pour in. They're reputation blossomed. The DuPont's had come.

Knowing where he'd come from, Big Bear would be damned of he allowed Mark to distort his creation. He would rather die! Three of his close friends were killed by the hands of Mark. Fred, Spank, and his dear brother, *Bull*. Learning of Mark's involvement in these murders drove him over the edge.

How could Mark be so cold to kill his own father?

This bothered him. He wanted revenge. He needed revenge. He didn't care that Mark was his nephew.

That nigga killed my brother.

His own father. So he could only imagine what Mark would do when it came to him.

Big Bear had spies everywhere, informants who came to him with information at all costs. So when Mark told him he was out of town, he knew he was lying. Mark was actually lying low somewhere in Brooklyn, trying to keep a low profile. Big Bear didn't get the actual address of where he was hiding yet, but when he did, he would be paying Mark a personal visit. Mark would be the first murder he committed since his return to the free world, he promised himself. It was time to get the clan back in order. Back to how it was supposed to be.

Straight like that!

Chapter 5

Lady decided to hit up the mall to get a few items for a trip she had planned. This would be her first time going out to Los Angeles and she wanted to have some fly wears for the occasion. Making it to a shopping center downtown Manhattan, she entered the establishment, running into a girl she knew from Harlem who was heading out.

"Lady, what's up?" asked Cora.

"Oh shit. What's up with you? Long time no see?" said Lady.

Cora used to be a part of her team, which consisted of Jamie and a few other girls. Rough around the edges, Cora was more on the tomboy side. In the facial department, she wasn't all that. Her figure resembled that of a little boy. She carried herself like a guy.

Cora joked, "I know. Ever since I moved on the eastside, y'all stopped checking for me."

"You damn right about that. I'm a westside girl. What I look like on the eastside."

The two laughed.

"What you into now?" Lady asked Cora.

Raising two shopping bags she was carrying, Cora smirked.

"Boasting."

"Still?" Lady asked with raised brows.

Cora had sticky-fingers since they were young. A certified kleptomaniac, she was always stealing something. Ever since junior high school she'd been a thief, and it was obvious nothing had changed.

Cora said, "All day. It pays the bills."

"I feel you on that."

"What you came here for? Anything you need I can get you if you like."

Lady wouldn't dare put her friend in a position to end up in jail. Taking up Cora's offer was out of the question. That wasn't her style. Maybe one time she would have jumped at the offer, but not now.

"Nah, I'm good. I'm a just run in and grab a few things," she said.

"I'm coming with you," volunteered Cora.

"You could roll if you want."

Making way to the Gucci store, Lady went to the footwear section, zeroing in on some loafers. *Those shits is hot.*

The price tag on them were $1500.

"Those shits is expensive, b," voiced Cora.

Lady laughed.

"Not really."

She called over a store clerk to assist with the purchase. She was sold on the shoes.

"Yes. Can I help you?" asked a Caucasian lady.

"Do you have any other colors in these shoes?" She pointed at the loafers.

"Yes. There's black, white, green, and dark blue."

"Oh, wow." Lady looked up at the ceiling to calculate some numbers in her head, then said, "Let me get all of them."

"All of them?" asked Cora and the store clerk at the same time, both wearing shocked expressions.

Lady looked at the two as if they were crazy.

"Yeah. What's the problem?"

"No problem," replied the store clerk politely. "Can you tell me your shoe size?"

"I wear a size four."

"Okay. I'll be right back."

When the clerk walked off, Cora got to talking in a whisper.

"That's damn near seven thousand when you add taxes for those shoes. This is Gucci; as a boaster, I can't even get those." She gestured toward the displayed shoes Lady sent for. "Gucci's security is way too tight."

"Okay. What's your point?" asked Lady, going in her pocket, taking out a large coil of cash.

Cora looked at the knot with wide eyes.

"You gotta tell me what you're into, girl. I need to get down."

Lady smiled. Before she got to respond, the store clerk came over with her shoes, four boxes stacked on top of each other.

"Would you like to try them on?"

"Nope. Just ring me up."

The trio went over to a cash register.

Lady's bill came out to $7100. Quickly counting out the cash, she handed the lady the money in all hundreds.

"Thanks for your business," smiled the lady.

"You're welcome."

When Lady left the Gucci store, she hit up quite a few other brand name stores in the mall, purchasing over fifteen thousand dollars in merchandise. Throughout the whole shopping trip, Cora kept making mention of how expensive the items she was buying were until she finally had enough and checked her.

"Listen, man, I get money. All these things that I'm buying does not even cost a fraction of what I make. I don't even lose a penny with these things."

She could tell Cora was embarrassed but she didn't care. Cora was talking too much, anyhow, and needed to know the real deal.

"Okay, girl. You got it," submitted Cora. "All I'm saying is that I want to get down with you. Whatever you got going on. I'm tired of boasting. I got two court cases for this shit, b. I wish I had the money to come in and buy shit like you."

Ignoring Cora, Lady continued her stroll through the mall in silence until reaching her final store, Lord and Taylor. Searching through the prominent chain for some under garments, someone bumped into her very hard causing her to drop her bags.

"What the fuck?!" she blurted out, looking from her bags on the floor to the person who bumped into her.

It was a man, much older than herself.

"You didn't see me, nigga?"

The man responded, "I been seen you, bitch! And if I wasn't in this mall, I would put a bullet through you."

The man paused to see if Lady would say something.

"You walking around without ya bodyguards like you ain't kill my people," he further stated.

Obviously, the man was a foe. Probably one of the guys from the Bronx. His words revealed this. Lady kept her cool, nevertheless. She was not scared or nervous. Outside, she had a car full of Young Gunners waiting on her return. Also, she carried a small .22 Caliber pistol. Staring back at the man, she was unfazed by his tough demeanor.

"What the fuck you mean, nigga?!" Cora spoke up, getting in the way of Lady, facing the man. "You got a problem with my friend?!"

Everyone in the store looked toward the commotion.

"Come outside. You'll see if I got a problem," the man replied.

"If there's a problem, let's do it right here. Why we gotta go outside?"

Lady grabbed at Cora's arm, pulling her friend away.

"Let's go outside like he said," she said, knowing her men were waiting on her.

Cora pulled away from Lady.

"Nah, fuck that! This nigga think he tough. What's up?" she tossed her bags on the floor. "Let's fight, nigga!"

The man cracked a smirk.

"Just come outside," he stated calmly, turning to walk away.

In a rage, Cora swung at the man, rocking his jaw.

He quickly spun around to take her on, swinging back, connecting with her face. The blow was a fierce one, but nothing to floor Cora. She ate it like a champ.

They went back-and-forth, throwing powerful blows at one another.

Lady, sneaking up as he fought with Cora, punched the man in the back of his head. He turned to face her, but she didn't back down. Almost instantly, she swung again, punching him square in the nose.

He moved for her.

Guarding her face in an attempt to block a sure collision with one of the man's fists, Lady was surprised when he suddenly fell to the floor, hit by something from behind.

What the fuck?

During Lady's bout, Cora snuck off to get a metal clothes rod to hit the man with, *an achieved feat.* Successfully striking her target, she stood above her prey with the rod like a champion after a victory.

They, *both*, then went to work on the floored man, stomping on him, kicking him all over the body. Not giving him the slight of chance to get up.

The melee went on for some time until security rushed in, pulling the girls off the man.

Cora screamed, "You bitch ass nigga!" as the security tried restraining her.

Lady kept calm as the security held onto her. She had a gun on her person and didn't want them to find it. Hopefully, they would just let her go. She surely hoped they did.

The man the girls had beaten, in a daze, got up from the floor. Wobbling in place, he spat out blood from his mouth. His face was swollen from the beating. He looked in bad shape.

Cora continued to carry on until Lady gave her an eye.

"Chill," she said, hoping Cora would get herself under control. Thankfully, she did, following Lady's command.

"What is the issue about?" one security guard asked.

"Just a misunderstanding," Lady spoke up before Cora or the man got the chance. "We're good."

"Are you sure? Can we let you guys out of here without further incident?"

"Absolutely," Lady answered first again.

"How about you guys?" asked the security, turning to Cora and the man that got beat down.

"I'm good," answered Cora.

"I'm cool," answered the man.

Once the security figured things were calm, he instructed the trio to pick up their property and exit the mall.

Wasting no time, Lady retrieved her bags and shot outside, followed by Cora.

"You a wild bitch," laughed Lady as she walked for the exit of the mall.

"I wasn't just gonna stand there and make that nigga mouth off," replied Cora. "That nigga had better know who he was talking to."

"You always been crazy, girl."

"And I'm crazier now."

Making it outside the mall, Lady walked to a caravan with Shooter Sean and two Young Gunners inside.

Lady said, "Get in. I'm a drop you home."

Leaving Cora behind was not an option, regardless of even how her friend felt about the situation. It was a possibility the man they assaulted was still around, waiting with his friends to get revenge. Thus, she would not risk Cora's life for a problem she got her into.

Cora got in the car with no protest.

The car pulled off when they were securely inside.

Lady explained to Shooter Sean what happened inside the mall.

"What?" he asked in surprise. "Let's go back and get that nigga."

"Nah. After what me and Cora did to him, I don't think he wants any more problems. We fucked that nigga up, b."

"Damn, man. I wish I went in there with you. My mind told me to go in with you, too." Shooter Sean punched at the air, upset.

"Don't worry about it. We put that work in."

Reaching 119th Street, the ride stopped in front a brownstone where Cora lived. There were some guys outside her building scoping their ride. All wore jackets with the words *The Mob* written on the back.

Shooter Sean knew one of the men, who called to him.

The guy called, "Yo, Shooter!"

"You know that nigga?" Lady asked, looking out the window at the man.

"Yeah. That's a DuPont. They call him Brick, the boss of The Mob crew from Harlem. He fucked with Kevin heavy. He stays out here on the eastside, though," answered Shooter Sean. "He's cool."

"Come, let me talk to you," Brick called.

Shooter Sean and Cora got out the car together.

"I'm a see you around, Lady," said Cora, walking off to her building.

Something seemed strange with Cora, Lady thought. They hadn't seen each other in so long, had just put in work on a nigga, and Cora had not even attempted to ask for her number. She did not know what to think of the situation, but let her go, deciding to let time be the judge.

Watching the men talk, she placed her hand on the pistol in her pocket. Brick looked like the bully type, big in size, with one of the meanest faces she'd ever saw. His roaming eyes made it seem like he was up to no good.

Rolling the window down, slightly, Lady listened in on the conversation.

"But you supposed to know not to get involved in DuPont business," Brick checked Shooter Sean. "It don't matter that you following orders from Drac. He's in jail, and only a DuPont on the outside supposed to *always* run shit."

Shooter Sean was clearly unfazed by Brick's hulky demeanor. Clearly, he respected the man, but did not fear him. He held his confidence as he made note that he was taking orders from Drac, *his boss*.

"I don't even like how you coming at me, Shooter,'" said Brick.

One of Brick's men made a funny move, readying Lady for some action. She took out her strap, resting it on her lap.

"Be on point," she said to the other man in the car. "It looks like something's about to go down, b."

"As I said, I follow Drac's rules and that's it," protested Shooter Sean, calmly.

Brick's man slipped a gun from the small of his back, catching Lady's attention. She quickly rolled the window all the way down.

"Have it your way then, b," voiced Brick, shrugging his shoulders while moving off a bit to the side.

His man quickly elevated his weapon.

BANG!

A shot tore through Brick's gunman shoulder, sending his gun falling to the ground.

Lady shot him just as he was about to shoot Shooter Sean.

Brick looked her way in shock, quickly dispersing inside a building, along with his other friends.

The one who was shot tried running, also, but Shooter Sean gunned him down, shooting him all over the body before racing back to the car.

"Drive off, b," Shooter Sean instructed the driver in a haste tone.

Adrenaline rushed through Lady as he thought about what just happened. Did she really just shoot somebody?

Yes, I did.

She had to, or else Shooter Sean would have possibly been killed. There was no way she could allow that to happen. Not on her watch. However, she was a bit shocked. Reflecting on aiming out the window and pulling the trigger, watching a bullet from her weapon enter the victim, gave her an adrenaline rush. She'd popped her cherry with shooting a nigga.

"You good?" she asked Shooter Sean.

"Yeah, b. Thank you so much," said Shooter Sean. "I would a woke up in heaven if it wasn't for you."

Though Shooter Sean made a joke about the matter, Lady didn't laugh. He surely would have been a dead man had she not reacted in the manner she had. Basically, he owed her his life.

"Shoot over to the projects. We gotta get low," she instructed.

"Say no more, b."

Chapter 6

Time for some action!

Mark loved this part best about the streets. Besides getting to some money, he found a thrill in laying his thug game down. He was a gangster and wanted people to know that. That's how it's always been. So when a female, *out of all people*, tested his gangster, he had to show out. He had to let a bitch know she wasn't on his level. For years he'd been on the streets, standing firm as a DuPont. Though his gangster had been questioned in the past, it had never been by a chick.

Who the fuck that bitch think she is?

Just thinking about a non-descript female ordering hits on his troops angered him every time. A bitch should have known better. But Lady didn't and she would have to pay for it.

"There that bitch go right there," gestured Donovan from the passenger seat of a ride he and Mark was in.

A woman exited a bar in the Sugar Hill section of Harlem, in a drunken stupor. Wobbling as she moved to the street to wave down a taxi. Intelligence had reached Mark's ear that the pub would be the women's whereabouts for the night, and he shot right over. There was no way he would miss the opportunity of getting a hold of the lady, who happened to be Lady's mother.

Putting the car in gear, he drove to where she was.

Donovan rolled down the window to speak with the woman.

"You need a ride?"

Looking in Donovan's direction, the woman stuck up a middle-finger.

"Do I look like I need a ride?" she asked in a slur.

There were people out on the street holding conversations, not paying much attention to what was going on. Everyone was in their own world.

Donovan quickly opened his door, hopping out just as fast. Everybody now watched, but he didn't care. Taking out a gun, he put it to the drunk woman. Grabbing her arm, he pulled her to the car.

Frightened, the woman looked at Donovan as if she saw a ghost. Then, in a shriek, she screamed out, *"Help!"*

She had everyone's attention, but her screams fell on deaf ears. No one could save her now.

Donovan slapped her with the pistol, knocking her out completely. Opening the rear door of the ride, he shoved her inside, getting in behind her.

Mark drove off right as the two got in. Racing through the Harlem streets, he made it to Edgecombe Avenue. Finding a park, he got out the car with Donovan.

The woman was knocked out in the backseat.

"I'm gonna let my niggas bring her to one of the apartments," said Donovan.

"Say no more," said Mark.

Donovan went inside a building to get some of his people.

Standing outside, Mark surveyed the block.

People were out and about. Hustlers bussed sales up-and-down the strip. Cars rode by, some blasting music. Harlem was looking like Harlem. The number one black community in New York, in Mark's eyes at least. Bronx was his first love, but then came Harlem. Just as he grew up in the boogie down, so he had in Harlem. Both boroughs were home.

Two men came out the building Donovan entered, going over to Mark's car. One man took the woman out, tossing her over his shoulder, while the next watched the streets as if to see everything was cool.

Donovan came to the building door and waved Mark over.

Heading inside the building, Mark was led to an apartment filled with Jamaicans. Instantly, he felt very uncomfortable but kept his cool. Donovan would not bring him anywhere where he would face harm.

The woman was placed on a shabby couch.

"Wake that bitch up!" Donovan instructed one of his soldiers, a boy who looked to be no more than thirteen.

Moving off to a kitchen area, the boy came back with a pot of water. Walking over to the woman, he tossed the water in her face.

She woke up right away.

Puzzled, she looked around at everybody.

"Who are you guys?" she asked, now seemingly sober.

Placing a chair before the woman, Donovan took a seat, staring her deep in the eyes.

"Where does your daughter live?" he asked.

Clearly scared, the woman went silent.

Hopping to his feet, Donovan stood before the woman.

"If I ask you again, you're not gonna like it," he warned.

"I really don't know," said the woman, now realizing the danger she was in. She began to cry.

Grabbing the woman by the shirt collar, Donovan ripped her shirt open, revealing a set of perky breasts.

Dark complexioned, the woman possessed a pretty face. Slim in figure, her body was well kept for her age.

"You're playing with me?" Donovan asked, picking up the woman from her seated position.

"No. I really don't know!" she cried.

Donovan punched her dead in the face, knocking her back on the couch. He then began to take off her clothes.

Mark wanted to intervene. One thing about the DuPont's, the family was against taking advantage of women. *This was blatant advantage.* Looking around the room at the other men present, he noticed they all wore smiles as if they were used to this behavior from their boss. It was clear the scene was nothing new to them.

"Chill, Donovan," he spoke up.

Everyone looked his way, *along with Donovan.*

"Chill?" Donovan asked, continuing to strip the lady completely naked. "I'm a show you chill."

Pulling the woman up from off the couch, he looked in her frightened face.

"My friend said to chill."

Roughly turning her around, he forced her back forward so that she was bending over, revealing her buttocks. Zipping down his zipper, he took out his erect penis.

"You said to chill, right?" he asked Mark, looking over at the man. "I'm a show you chill."

He forced his dick inside the woman, going as far as he could go.

"*Aggh!*" she screamed out in agony.

Holding the back of her neck, Donovan continued to watch Mark as he fucked the shit out of her.

"Spanglers don't chill," he said, pumping harder-and-harder. "Right guys?" he looked over at his friends.

"Spanglers don't chill!" shouted the men in unison, excitedly.

Mark was now nervous, fearful that he had rubbed Donovan the wrong way. Usually the man took his advice, but now he seemed to be in a zone. While Donovan fucked the lady, he watched him, looking as if he was coming for him next. The woman's screams made things more terrifying. Mark's heart pounded in his chest, but he kept a straight face. He knew if he made it out of this, he would never fuck with Donovan again. Raping the lady was uncalled for. He would have rather they just killed her. However, Donovan had broken a sacred rule in the DuPont clan.

Never rape a woman!

Thinking back, his father would repeat this over-and-over.

"If the bitch don't want to give you the pussy, move on to the next bitch," Bull would say.

Mark lived by this and would never break the code.

When Donovan got through with the woman, he let his crew have their way with her, also.

Mark couldn't take it no more. He left the apartment.

Donovan followed him out.

"Man, Donovan, I'm not with that rape shit, man," he said, shaking his head, standing in the building halls with the Jamaican.

"Let me tell you something," started Donovan, staring straight into Mark's eye, "never *you* have mercy on a nigga or bitch. That bitch in there has to pay for what her daughter did. And if she don't turn over the information we need, I'm a kill her."

Seeing no use in debating with Donovan, Mark put his hands up.

"You got it, nigga. Just do what you gotta do. But I'm a wait outside. I don't wanna see all that shit."

"I'll be out shortly," Donovan agreed.

Walking out the building, Mark tried keeping a low profile. He didn't want anyone to notice him, so he leaned up on a wall and pulled a hoodie over his head. Two men walked his way, *probably Jamaicans*, while three women talked loud on the block on the other side of the street. Keeping a hand close to his waist where a pistol rested, he side-eyed the men who were getting close. When they got closer, he realized they were not Jamaicans by their accents. They sounded American. For the split of a second, he looked off at the women across the street.

The move cost him.

One of the men ran up on him, grabbing his arm near his pistol. The other stood before him with a huge smile planted on his face.

Oh shit!

Realizing who it was, he knew he was in for a ride.

"Don't struggle, nigga," said Big Bear. "Calm yourself."

Looking everywhere for assistance from the Jamaicans, none was in sight. Mark was doomed, wondering if he was set up by Donovan.

Big Bear shook his head.

"You're really looking for their help, huh? From the same motherfuckers *you* used to set up my son, huh?" he asked when noticing Mark searching for help.

A loud *BOOM* sounded off, causing the man holding Mark to loosen his grip.

Big Bear looked toward the building Mark exited a few minutes earlier. A man, holding a smoking pistol, looked his way with an angry expression. Sprinting behind a car, Big Bear, and his cohort, backed out pistols and got to shooting.

It sounded like M80 fireworks going off. Multiple at a time. Cars drove up on the scene, armed men alighted from them, joining in on the gunfight. All were apart of Big Bear's crew and meant business.

Dodging a few bullets, Mark dashed to safety, making it inside a storefront on the street. The clerk behind the store's counter got low right as he entered the establishment, *frightened*. Heading to the back of the store, Mark stooped low, gripping his exposed pistol. If someone came inside that seemed like a threat, he would send them to their maker.

Outside, the shots continued. Big Bear meant business. He didn't come to play. Luckily, Mark escaped the first round of his terror. A whole lot more would follow, he knew.

Now he knew for sure Big Bear wanted his life. Just the thought was scary. Being on the other side of Big Bear's gun was not a pleasant thing. His uncle would stop at nothing to kill an enemy. This he knew for sure.

Finally, the shots stopped. Car tires squalled aloud as they raced off the scene. Police sirens wailed.

Mark, cautiously, made way to the front of store. Gun in hand. He would not get caught slipping. Pulling the store's door open to go outside, he looked out first. The coast seemed clear, so he walked out.

People were everywhere. Eyes searched the street, possibly for a reemergence of Big Bear and his crew.

Mark noticed Donovan standing with his men. He quickly went over to the Jamaican.

"That nigga almost killed me, man," said Mark, thinking of how close his uncle got to taking him out.

Visibly angry, Donovan ignored Mark. He kept looking back at the building.

Following Donovan's eyes, Mark noticed a woman near the entrance to the building he was in earlier, lying on the ground. *Dead.*

Donovan finally spoke up.

"They killed my sister, man," he said, shaking his head.

People guarded the body of the female. The girls who were across the street earlier were present, surrounding the victim, shedding tears of sorrow.

"I'm so sorry for your lost, man," said Mark, knowing Donovan must have felt fucked up about what happened to his sister. With all that was going on, though, he had to get out of dodge. He did not want to be around when the police showed up. "I'm a make a move."

Donovan shook his head.

Mark went to his car, got inside, and sped off the scene.

Chapter 7

Big Bear usually didn't miss a mark. This time, though, he had when Mark escaped a sure death sentence. He had Mark right where he wanted him but somehow, he slipped through the cracks.

Fuck!

This infuriated Big Bear. He could not get over what had taken place.

He had no intentions of running into Mark on Edgecombe Avenue. The mission was to catch some Jamaicans slipping, send them off to heaven or hell, then get out of dodge. It was important that he set an example. However, he caught sight of Mark, which totally changed the initial plan. Stepping right to business, he instructed a henchman to grab hold of Mark so that he didn't get away. When he did, all hell broke loose. One of the Jamaicans stepped outside a building firing a gun, causing him to react. During his reaction, Mark got away.

Back in control of the family, Big Bear mounted a line of troops from all over the city. He had Harlem, Queens, Bronx, Staten Island, and Brooklyn gangsters on payroll. His army spoke for itself. Once again, he'd become a powerful force in the streets. His intentions. He'd been gone long enough and needed everyone to know he was back.

Dressed in a dark blue suit, a trench coat, and some gators, it was time to attend a family meeting. From the circumference of a pub he owned in Harlem, he would address everyone about what had been going on in the streets. Stepping out his Polo Grounds apartment, he was met by a few bodyguards.

"What's going on?" he greeted the men, who in return gave head nods of acknowledgements.

Catching the elevator, Big Bear noticed some graffiti in the shaft.

The Young Gunners.

Someone had left their mark, spray painting their gang on the wall.

Drac's gang.

The crew of thugs ran rampant through Harlem, laying it down in the name of the DuPont's, Big Bear acknowledged. But he was home now, and no longer needed their assistance. He'd assembled troops who would bring the family back to its grace. Nevertheless, if he needed assistance from the Young Gunners, they were only a phone call away. Shooter Sean was always around, Drac's friend whom he had a somewhat relationship with.

Stepping out the elevator on the first floor, Big Bear was met by a few more soldiers. Usually, when he hit the streets, he kept some goons around, but, really, didn't need no one's assistance outside. He could hold his own, as he had always done during his come up. Before the street fame, bodyguards, and everything else that came along with running shit, Big Bear moved alone. Even with bodyguards, he moved as if he was by himself, making it hard for even his bodyguards to keep up with him at times.

Community residents came up to Big Bear out on the courtyard of Polo Grounds, acknowledging him with smiles, asking for favors, and just for handshakes. There were a lot of new people around since he left, but many, from his day, was still around. While his bodyguards surveyed the scene, keeping an eye on the atmosphere, Big Bear greeted the people. It was very important to keep a good relationship with residents in the community, he knew. By treating the neighborhood good, he would get the needed assistance if ever something arose that could be detrimental to his well-being.

"Hey, Pat," Big Bear greeted a woman he knew from his start in Polo Grounds. He and the lady were very close friends along the years. She held him down when shit got sticky on quite a few occasions.

"What's going on, Big Bear?" said Pat. "Let me hold something."

Big Bear smiled.

"You know you could get anything from me. Anytime. What you need?"

"I really need a washing machine. Before they killed Kevin, he promised me one."

As usual, Big Bear became somber when hearing his son's name.

Why Pat had to bring that up?

Nevertheless, if his son promised someone something before his death, Big Bear wanted to assist with Kevin keeping his word. *Even in his death.*

Dipping in his pocket, he took out a knot of cash. Counting off a few bills, he handed it to Pat.

"If you need more, let me know," he said before walking off.

It was time to get to his family. To handle business. Nothing came before handling business. It was very important to keep on top of things on the journey to success. Big Bear learned this as a youth and stuck to these rules. This was one of the main reasons why he was so successful in life. He stuck with regimen, even when he didn't feel like doing so. He taught his sons these qualities, and because of that, they grew up to be successful boys.

Reaching the pub, the place was crowded with family members. People he hadn't seen in ages came out. Aunts, uncles, cousins, other relatives. The family had grown, also, Big Bear noticed. The offspring of family members crowded the bar. He was introduced to so many new family that he couldn't keep count. The DuPont's were definitely in the building.

One man stood out among the crowd. Big Bear, with no shade, penetrated the man with a serious eye. His focus caused everyone to look the man's way. Then he walked over to the man, staring him deep in the eyes.

"Who side are you on?" he wanted to know.

If the man gave a wrong answer, he would kill him in front of everyone.

It was Bull's younger son, Bill, who carried the same build as his father and serious expression. Big Bear heard Bill and Mark were partners in business and were making lots of money together. Thus, his loyalty probably was with his brother. If this was the case, Bill was pretty much a dead man.

The atmosphere became quiet as everyone watched the scene.

Bill kept a straight face as he addressed Big Bear.

"That's not even a question to ask, unc.' I'm on the family's side," he responded with surety in his tone.

"So is your brother. But he's trying to take over the family."

"I'm not on what Mark is on, Big Bear. I have respect for you and the entire family. I don't support what he's done and what he's doing. I haven't been in communication with him for some time now."

Staring deep into Bill's eyes, Big Bear looked for signs of deceit. He couldn't see anything in Bill's eyes, so he walked off without a word. However, he would keep an eye on Bill, and would instruct everyone else to keep a close watch on the man, also.

"Big Bear," called a man. "I really need to speak with you."

Stopping to speak with Brick, a cousin who'd done lots of dirt with him in the streets, he wondered why the man was so anxious to talk.

"What's going on?" he asked.

"My nigga, Drac's bitch, Lady, gotta die, man," said Brick. "She killed one of my soldiers for no reason."

There were so many tales of Lady. Big Bear heard so much about the woman, mainly stories about her defending the family's name. She'd become a godmother in Harlem, a black widow to some. Big Bear had yet to meet her, and actually didn't care to meet her.

"What you mean?"

"She came on the block and just opened fire on me and my crew."

"Just like that?" Something seemed fishy to Big Bear.

"Just like that, family. The bitch is outta control. She gotta die, man."

"So you're saying that she just pulled up on your block and opened fire? *She* was the trigger man?"

"Yes, Big Bear, she was the one shooting," answered Brick with surety.

Big Bear read Bricks body language. Something was off but he couldn't pinpoint it. There was really nothing he could do about Brick's complaint now, so he would have to get back to the issue. One thing for sure, though, he'd never heard that Lady was firing guns. Her skillset was, strategically, sending off troops to handle business.

"I'll get back to you about this," he said, walking off to another section of the pub.

Making his rounds, he acknowledged everyone with handshakes and hugs before getting up on a stage at the head of the gathering. Gesturing for everyone to quiet up, he began to speak.

"I would like to thank everyone for coming out," he started. "It's a pleasure to be in the presence of so many DuPont's. Both young-and-old. This is my first-time meeting some of you guys, but, trust, the DuPont energy could be felt in our embrace. This was how our ancestors left it to be."

Big Bear watched the gathering as he spoke.

"We are a family, the strongest in Harlem. Maybe the city. And we *must* keep things that way. We can't allow anything to get in between that. It's DuPont or nothing."

Getting deeper into his spill, Big Bear went on to speak on Mark's disloyalty and the urgency in the matter.

"He is one of us, but he has strayed. And we can't have that."

He let everyone know his feelings towards Mark, that he wanted him dead.

"If anyone has an issue with that, step forward now."

Waiting on anyone to step forward, Big Bear continued his speech when no one stepped up.

"We're gonna continue to run shit; to buy all the property we can; own all the businesses we can; take over as many blocks as we can. We are the meaning of black success and will continue to strive to be the best to ever do it."

After his speech, Big Bear met with a few of his cousins, the most serious out the pack, which included Brick. These were his killing machines, the ones he could count on to lay shit down.

"We know what we gotta do, so let's get to it," said Big Bear. "Mark has to die. I'm giving you guys forty-eight hours to get to him. Bring him to the Bear Cave naked and dead."

Everyone present shook their heads, knowing what they had to do.

"We'll be in touch," said Big Bear, leaving the pub.

Chapter 8

Lady felt like the world was on her shoulders. She was beyond stressed. Finally, she got a call that her mother's body was found. It came as no surprise, though. She expected to receive the daunting news. Her mother had left the house days before, claiming to be headed to her boyfriend's pad.

"Be careful out there, mom," Lady had said.

"I've been doing this street shit long before you were born, girl," was the last words she heard from her mother before she left the house for good.

The day, Lady felt kind of funny. Something came over her; it was like she knew something bad was going to happen. But couldn't put a finger on it. When the night manifested itself and she didn't hear from her mother, she reached out to her boyfriend.

"She got drunk, flipped out on me, and went to a bar," said her mother's boyfriend.

"What bar?" Lady asked.

"This spot in Sugar Hill."

Obviously, someone picked her up after the bar, brought her somewhere, raped her, tortured her, and disposed of her body, throwing her in the center of the FDR where she was run over by multiple moving cars. Thinking of the gruesome nature of her mother's death made Lady shed a tear. Someone had violated in the worst way.

But who?

This played over-and-over in her head. Who could have done such a horrible thing to her mother? Why? It could have been Lady's actions in the streets that got her mother killed. Lady would not leave this out. There were many individuals who wanted her dead and would stop at nothing to bring her pain. This she understood. If this was the case, though, all rules were broken when they killed her mother. Certain people were to be left out the fighting in the streets, or so she believed in the past. Now she realized that all was fair in war.

She could not just sit around the house and be stressed about what occurred. It was a must that she got herself in order. Calling Shooter Sean, she told him to come and get her. She wanted to get some fresh air.

"What you feel like getting into?" asked Shooter Sean, once retrieving Lady near her house.

He came with one of his underbosses, Bert, a small-framed gunner from Harlem.

"Let's head out to the Rucker Park. Probably there's a game or something going on out there," said Lady, resting back in the car seat, trying to clear her head.

"I think there's a celebrity match going on there today," said Bert, driving the car they all were in.

"That's good," said Lady.

The trio drove to Harlem. Making it to their destination, they parked the ride and got out the car.

Lady noticed a large crowd in Rucker Park. People from all walks of life came out to witness the current match up, clearly. Whites; Blacks; Asians; Arabians; countless nationalities crowded the park.

People from the neighborhood acknowledged Lady with various gestures of respect. Meeting up with a pack of Young Gunners, she went to a section in the park occupied mainly by people from Polo Grounds.

"This joint is packed, b," said Shooter Sean, standing next to Lady at the forefront of the Young Gunners.

Lady shook her head. Folding her arms across her chest, she watched her surroundings. Things could easily get crazy with the amount of people present, so she stayed on point. Eyes everywhere watched her; she matched every stare. She didn't know who to trust, especially after the death of her mother. Until she found out the culprits responsible for her mother's death, everyone was a suspect. The button could be pressed on anyone.

A DJ played music in the park in between intermissions of the game. Cheerleaders danced about in skimpy outfits. The scene was something to talk about.

"*Oh shit!*" shouted the DJ. "*Oh shit!*"

A crowd entered the park, catching everyone's attention.

"Salute to the king of Harlem!" praised the DJ.

Just as herself, Lady noticed Shooter Sean watching a gang of goons entering the park, led by none other than Big Bear.

Walking with a swag of command and confidence, Big Bear moved like the boss he was. This was the first time Lady saw him since she was younger. Besides gaining a couple extra pounds, he looked the same. His face spelled *dangerous*. It was obvious that he was not to be fucked with.

"That's the nigga Brick with him," whispered Shooter Sean to Lady.

Lady had already caught sight of Brick. Her hand moved to a tote bag she was carrying when she noticed Big Bear moving her way with his gang of thugs. She noticed Shooter Sean's hand shooting to his waist where a pistol laid.

"Shout out to the Big Bear of Harlem," said the DJ right before dropping a joint by a famous rapper supposedly made about Big Bear.

Big Bear walked right up to Lady.

"Donna's daughter," he said, wearing a smirk.

Keeping an eye on Big Bear, Lady also watched the men he was with, *especially Brick*, whose face looked as if he tasted something sour.

"Yes," she responded.

"You don't remember me?"

"Yes." *Of course I do.*

"So you're my son's wife? I heard a lot about what you've done for my family."

Lady just shook her head. She did not know what else to say. With what she was going through with the death of her mother, and by the way Brick was screw facing her, she felt like exploding. She really regretted coming to the park.

"I heard about your mother. And I'm sorry for your loss," said Big Bear in a sincere tone. "The Jamaicans are responsible for that. I already got intel on it."

Big Bear's information peaked Lady's interest. Hearing that the Jamaicans were responsible for her mother's death brought on a new anger within. She wanted to ask him if he was sure but remembered who Big Bear was. He knew everything. People volunteered information to him for no reason at all.

"We're definitely gonna get some get back for that, but, in the meantime, you stay out of the neighborhood," warned Big Bear. "I'm gonna give you a pass on what you did to my family here soldier." He gestured toward Brick. "That's your pass."

It took everything in Lady's power to not respond to Big Bear. She just watched, allowing him to talk.

Big Bear waved his hand at Lady, Shooter Sean, and the Young Gunners.

"Y'all get out the park," he ordered.

All the Young Gunners looked toward Lady and Shooter Sean before moving, as if asking what they should do. Most of the boys were young, and actually didn't know Big Bear. They'd only heard of him but never seen him before.

Embarrassed, Lady led the charge, walking for the park's exit. With her troops, she could take on Big Bear, and maybe even win, but such a thing was too risky. So she took the high road, leaving the park, followed by Shooter Sean and the rest of the gang.

"*Pussy, nigga!*" someone shouted to Lady's rear, which was followed by a loud *BANG!*

Someone fired a shot.

Taking a quick glimpse over her shoulder, Lady saw Brick with a smoking pistol, aimed her way. On the ground next to her lied Shooter Sean with a fresh bullet wound to the head.

Big Bear had set her up. Breaking into flight mode, she got low as Brick began to fire more shots at her and the Young Gunners.

People ran everywhere in the park, in search of cover. Shots rang out all over now. It was more than just Brick shooting. The scene became chaotic.

Dashing outside the park, Lady ran for Polo Grounds. However, she stopped short when realizing she could be running into a death trap. Big Bear had proven that he was against her, so if she ran in the projects, she could be killed. Thus, she ran in another direction, moving away from the projects.

Making it a few blocks over, she stopped near a parked car to catch her breath. What had taken place was almost unbelievable. It was mere luck that she made it out the park. She was supposed to be dead like Shooter Sean.

Shooter Sean.

Thinking of her friend, she began to cry. He was no longer among the living and didn't deserve to go out the way he had. Shooter Sean had done so much for the DuPont family. There was no way he should have been taken out by them.

"*Fuck!*" she screamed out loud, beyond angry.

A car raced on the scene, coming to a screaming halt in front of her. Thinking it was Brick who had come to finish her off, she went to dive behind the car she was near. But it was Bert.

"Get in!" Bert called.

Lady quickly got in the ride.

Bert raced off.

"They killed my nigga, man," Bert said in a shaky voice. "I knew that fucker was gonna do something." He banged on the car wheel as he drove. "I seen it in his eyes, man."

As Bert vented, Lady sat in a daze. She was still in disbelief with what happened. Her life had literally flashed before her eyes. She'd never been so close to death. Even when she was shot before, she wasn't so close to death. This time was far different.

"You okay?" Bert asked.

"Yeah. I made it out," said Lady, coming to her senses a bit.

"That faggot killed Shooter Sean, man. I seen my nigga on the floor dead, b." Bert began to cry.

"Drop me off out in Queens." Lady wanted to go home.

First her mother killed, now Shooter Sean. Things had gotten too real. She needed some time to think.

"Say no more, b."

Chapter 9

The streets were flaming. Things had spiraled so far out of control that Mark decided to skip town for a bit, heading down to Miami. He needed some chill out time, away from everything. Keeping a low profile in his South Beach condo, he stayed indoors most of the time.

"Man, I need to come down there with you," said Bill over the phone. "Shit is crazy out here, man. Niggas is dying left-and-right. You done started some shit, bro."

Mark felt where his brother was coming from.

"Get on a flight and come down. You know you're always welcome here."

"I just might do that. The way this nigga Big Bear is moving is crazy. He really wants your head, and it's only a matter of time before he finds out that we're still connected."

Bill had informed Mark of what had taken place at the family meeting, that he had to lie to Big Bear about their relationship. If Bill had mentioned that he was still in touch with Mark, he probably would have been killed.

Hearing the pressure his brother was under, angered Mark. Big Bear was out of line.

"Fuck that nigga, bro. I don't fear that sucker," said Mark, meaning every word.

He was past tired of Big Bear's shit. If his uncle wanted a war, he was ready! Lines had been crossed, anyhow. There was no coming back over after all that had taken place.

"I'm with you on that. But that nigga got a large army out here."

"And so do we. That nigga can't fuck with us."

Big Bear surely had an army, but so did Mark. After the situation with Donovan, he kind of fell back from the Jamaican, but could still call on the man for anything. Especially laying a nigga down in the streets. He also had many shooters from the Bronx who were willing to put a bullet through a nigga for him. So Big Bear had a problem on his hands when it came to him.

"I feel you, bro," said Bill. "You know I got your back, regardless."

"I know that's without a question, bro."

Once Mark got through speaking with his brother, he decided to go out on the town to catch a bite on the strip. Putting a gun on his hip, he went outside.

Ocean Drive Boulevard was crowded with people, moving to-and-fro on the strip.

Pulling a hat low on his head, Mark maneuvered through the packed streets, making sure to stay alert as he did so. The current war had left him paranoid. Even though he was in Florida, that didn't mean he couldn't be touched. His family possessed riches, and it wouldn't take Big Bear nothing to pay someone to hit him anywhere he was on earth. Therefore, he stayed on his p's-and-q's.

Stopping at a taco spot, he ordered a few burritos. As he waited for his order, his eyes came upon a white man standing outside the establishment, looking his way.

Fuck he looking at?

Refraining from keeping eye contact with the man, he looked away. He did not want the man to notice that he was aware he was watching. When he got his order, he headed for the exit. A man who was sitting in the business got up as he was leaving out.

Something's up.

Outside, he walked for his place. The men were now following him. Sliding a hand down to his waist, he took his gun off his hip. A car came to a halt in the street before him just as he was about to spin and fire on the men following him.

Two men jumped out, flashing badges.

"Freeze! FBI!" shouted the man.

Stunned, Mark dropped his gun to the ground, along with his food. He placed his hands in the air.

The men who were following, had by now ran up on him, grabbing his arms.

"Hey, Mr. DuPont. You're caught," said the white man who was initially staring Mark down outside the taco spot.

Mark didn't know what was going on but knew he was caught red-handed with a firearm. That alone would get him some time in the big house. But why were the FEDS after him, he wondered. Did someone snitch about all that was going on in New York? Had he been spotted committing a crime? Confused, he let the FEDS take him in without resistance.

"That gun could put you away for some time, you know?" one federal agent asked Mark, sitting across from him in an interrogation room. "But we can make that disappear if you help us out."

Keeping the code of silence, Mark had no intentions of telling the FEDS anything. Yeah, he was caught with a gun, but *so…* If he had to sit up for the weapon, so be it. At least he would see some light at the end of the tunnel.

"I would like to see my lawyer, please," he said, staring across at the agent.

The agent cracked a smirk.

"You sure you wanna take it there?" he asked.

Shaking his head, Mark stared directly at the agent.

Matching his gaze, the agent penetrated Mark.

"I think you better help me out, so that I could help you out."

"Help me out?"

Fuck he talking 'bout?

"Do you think it's a coincident that we found you in Miami? This was planned."

The agent had Mark's attention. He was confused now.

The agent continued. "There's a lot of piled up murder cases awaiting you in New York," he said. "If we didn't catch you, and you made it back to New York, we would have gotten you as soon as you got off the plane. Don't think we arrested you for a measly gun."

Now Mark was nervous. One thing he didn't want to go to jail for was a body. They held you too long in the system for those type of charges. He could not see himself doing a life sentence. That was too much for him.

"So are you gonna help me or not? I don't want to be wasting my time," said the agent.

"Help you with what?" Mark wanted to know.

"With getting Big Bear, and his son, Drac, off the street *forever*. As I said, if you help me, I can help you. If you get those guys off the streets, it can help you to finally run the DuPont family."

"I don't know what you talking 'bout."

"Yes, you do."

There was no way Mark would snitch out his family, regardless of the situation going down in the streets. One of the most sacred rules in the family was that no one should snitch, *under no circumstances*. Right about now he hated Big Bear and Drac, but not enough to snitch on them.

Fuck that.

"Have it your way, then," said the agent. "You're under arrest for the unlawful possession of a firearm, and the murder of Kenny Wilson back in New York."

Kenny Wilson?

Mark couldn't pinpoint who that was. Committing so many murders along the years, sending out innumerable hits, he figured that could be anyone. Whoever it was, he was willing to sit down and wait on a judge to explain his charges.

Booked on weapon and murder charges, Mark was placed in a holding pen with other prisoners awaiting to be seen by a judge.

Finding a seat in the cramped cell, he let out a breath of stress. From being in an exclusive Miami condo to now in a jail, made his head hurt. Furthermore, he was in on some serious charges, infractions that could put him away for life.

Fuck!

"Yo, my man," called a Latino man, approaching Mark.

Looking around, Mark wondered if the man was talking to him. He pointed at himself to make sure.

"Yeah, you," confirmed the Latino man. "I need that seat."

One thing about Mark, he was no sucker. Coming from the Bronx, weakness was not in his blood. He was ready to get down. *Anytime. Any place.* That's just how he was raised. He eyed the man, who was about the same size as himself.

The Latino man asked, "You didn't hear me?"

"Loud and clear," said Mark, getting up from his seat.

Everyone in the cell watched the drama unfold.

Moving away to allow the man to sit, Mark coyly smirked when the Latino sat down.

"That's what I thought," smiled the Latino man, sitting in a victorious position, poking out his chest.

In a swift motion, Mark attacked the man, knocking him off the seat. Moving ahead with his attack, he got to stomping the man's head on the floor, beating him to a bloody pulp. One thing was for certain, as long as he was in jail, he would not allow anyone to punk him. As a Bronx bomber, he would stand his ground. *Every time.*

Chapter 10

Circling the streets of Harlem, Big Bear hunted Brick. He couldn't wait to get his hands on the man. The move Brick pulled in Rucker Park raised the hairs on his neck; he couldn't wait to put a bullet through his frame.

Shooter Sean was killed by the hands of Brick, along a few other innocent bystanders. The chaotic scene in Rucker Park played on the news for the past week, coupled with photos of a present Big Bear. Headlines read that he was responsible, which was far from the truth. He had not given Brick the greenlight to react in such a manner. *Brick pulled that move on his own*, unbeknownst to Big Bear. Had he had the slightest idea Brick would do such a dumb thing, he would have intervened. However, the worst had occurred, placing Big Bear, *once again*, in the hot seat.

He was wanted by the authorities for questioning but refused to turn himself in. Going back to prison was not an option. The cops would have to work to catch him.

Fuck that.

Two carloads of goons trailed his ride. He knew where to find Brick and anticipated pulling up on the man.

It was nighttime. The streets were quite empty. New York's brisky weather sent everyone in early.

But Big Bear was out. *Hunting.*

Palming a .357 Magnum, he steered his car with a free hand. The deadly pipe was his weapon of choice. He loved the size-holes it put through niggas. It was a must he put a few shots in Brick's face, sending him off in a closed casket. The man would learn, since he hadn't before, to never pull a stunt in his presence. What Brick did was a stunt. Killing Shooter Sean was uncalled for.

A stop light caught him at 119th. Watching his mirror, he made sure no one tried to sneak up on him. When the light changed, he turned on the block. Catching sight of Brick standing with a girl, he quickly pulled over near a fire hydrant.

Brick saw the cars enter the block and began to watch.

Big Bear and his entourage got out their cars, guns drawn, moving for Brick. Elevating his firearm, he was surprised to see Brick already had a gun out, positioning to raise it also. But before he got to squeeze, shots rang out, coming from somewhere on the block.

Dropping to the ground, Big Bear crawled to cover. Someone(s) was taking on him and his team. Getting behind a car, he searched the atmosphere to see who was shooting. Catching sight of a figure on a roof, he realized snipers were out, holding down the block. Aiming upwards at the roof, he let off a few rounds.

A few of his men were gunned down. Their bodies lied still in the street. Because of what was playing out, he had to get out of dodge. He'd fallen into a boobie trap. In a kneel position, he found his way back to his car under what seemed like raining gunshots. Managing to get inside, he hurried off the scene. Bullets battered his car, but he made it out alive.

Things had gotten out of hand within the family. Mark had taken on Big Bear, and now Brick. Such a thing could not have happened before.

It would not have happened.

Infuriated, Big Bear took a ride to lower Manhattan. He knew right where to go to make Brick feel it for his violation. Parking the ride on a back street in the Village, he put his gun on his waist and got out the car. Heading for a building, one he'd spent many a night in during his come up, he entered the domain, going up to an apartment on a second-floor level. Banging the door, a familiar lady answered.

"Oh shit, Big Bear," said Janet, his cousin.

Pushing his way inside Janet's apartment, he closed the door behind himself. Grabbing her by the hair, he dragged her petite, slim frame to her living room.

She screamed, "'Bear, why are you doing this?!"

Pulling his gun, Big Bear shoved it in Janet's face, breaking a few of her teeth during the process.

"Call your son now!" he barked.

"We can talk about this, 'Bear. What did he do?" cried Janet, blood dripping from her mouth, trying to calm Big Bear.

In his element of death, Big Bear didn't want to hear anything. His mind was made up. He was going to kill Janet. But before he did, he wanted to talk to Brick, her son, so that he could let the man know he was nothing to fuck with. While still holding Janet by the hair, his gun trained on her, he forced her over to a phone.

"Pick it up and call that nigga."

Janet quickly picked up the phone, dialing a number. Placing it to her ear, it rang a few times before Brick answered.

"Brick, Big Bear is gonna kill me. What did you do?" she cried into the phone.

"Fuck that nigga, mom! I'll handle him when I catch him," said Brick, loud enough for Big Bear to hear.

Pressing the trigger on his weapon, the magnum roared, exploding in Janet's face, blowing a hole through her. Loosening his grip on Janet, he let her drop to the ground. He could still hear Brick on the other end of the line, screaming his mother's name. Obviously, he'd heard the shot go off, as Big Bear intended for him to hear.

Fixing himself up, Big Bear left the apartment, closing the door behind himself.

Making way back to his car, he sat and waited. It would only be a matter of time before Brick showed up to investigate what happened to his mother. Big Bear would then put a bullet through him.

However, before Brick showed up, the police came on the scene, rushing inside the building.

Turning on the vehicle, Big Bear slowly drove off.

Chapter 11

"I still haven't heard from him to tell him a piece of my mind," voiced Drac, sitting on a visit floor with Lady.

"Boy, if it wasn't your father, I would tell you to let the dogs loose. He really violated," said Lady, thinking back to the day Shooter Sean was killed.

"Listen, man, fuck all that father shit. He's been ignoring me from the jump, so I don't care anymore about how he feels. Brick killed my friend, so he gotta go. Let the Young Gunners commit a double homicide for that."

"You sure, Drac?"

If Drac were to set the dogs loose, it would be as if he were going against his father, and Lady didn't know if she wanted to be a part of that.

Drac looked across the table at Lady.

"Listen, babe. You tell Bert and them to kill shit. And don't stop."

"Say no more, babe."

After the visit with Drac, Lady met up with Ms. Elma. The woman had been schooling her to the real estate game, opening her eyes to countless opportunities. Her mother's death affected her in the worst way but gave her the drive to get focused. Running around as the queen of Harlem would not matter if she didn't have anything to fall back on. As an official DuPont, she wanted to continue their tradition of being an owner of multiple properties and establishments. She wanted to set a solid foundation for herself, her unborn future children, and would do just that.

"Things have been heating up out here in the streets," said Ms. Elma from behind her office desk.

"Very much so," Lady responded.

Since her first house purchase, she and Ms. Elma built a tight bond. During the course of their new friendship, Lady learned the lady came upon the DuPont family by mere luck and became a millionaire over night because of the union. Big Bear had his eye on a particular property back in the day that he just had to get. Ms. Elma, an upcoming realtor at the time, had access to the listing of the property but already had someone in mind for the sell. However, a friend brought Big Bear to her, explaining his urgent interest in the property. He offered cash up front and promised an additional sum if he could get the property. Ms. Elma bit the bait. This move led to a union with the DuPont family and brought her in million's years to come.

"I just spoke to Big Bear a few days ago," said Ms. Elma. "Told him to keep his cool out here in the streets; things are not the same as back in the day. But if you know Big Bear, you will know that he doesn't listen to anyone but himself."

"I see," said Lady, shaking her head.

The incident in the park still played in her head. She wouldn't reveal how she felt about Big Bear to anyone, but she hated his guts. Because of him, Shooter Sean was killed, and an attempt was made on her life.

Ms. Elma got low on her desk, gesturing for Lady to get closer as if someone could hear them. They were the only two in the office, but, clearly, Ms. Elma wanted to be cautious with what she had to say about Big Bear.

She whispered, "He's not gonna last out here. The police are already looking for him."

Lady just shook her head. It was all over the news that the police were looking for Big Bear. There was no need for Ms. Elma to tell her this. She knew almost everything that was going on in Harlem. Furthermore, she didn't think that Ms. Elma should be talking about Big Bear either.

"Let's discuss business. I didn't come here to speak about Big Bear."

Lady's reaction caught Ms. Elma off guard; it showed in her face. But Lady did not care. Getting involved in the streets had taught her to always be serious. There was no time to be kidding around with anyone, even if a cool friendship existed. Business was business, and Lady was about her business.

"You're right, Lady. I'm so sorry. Let's get down to business," said Ms. Elma, beginning to rummage through some papers on her desk.

"Yeah, let's do that."

"There's four buildings for sale out in Brooklyn, the downtown area."

"Downtown Brooklyn? That's the slums." *Why would I want property there?*

"It surely is the slums, but it's an up-and-coming slum. Within the next twenty years, that neighborhood will experience an entirely different look and vibe. And these are the things you must stay focused on, grabbing property even in the slums. That's what the Jews are doing even now, buying up everything while the price is right. Pretty soon, you won't be able to get any property. Even the ones in the slums."

"So what's the price tag on these buildings now?"

"You can get all four of them with zero down, because your credit is so good, and get a mortgage on them. Or you can buy them out right for about four hundred k."

"Wouldn't buying them out right be the best option?"

"Yes. Because, if, by some chance, you don't have the money in the future to pay the mortgage, you can end up losing the properties. But if you buy them out right, they're yours."

"So let's do what's best. Let's get the money on them."

"Okay."

One of Lady's goals was to own property like Big Bear. She had enough money to begin her journey and was head strung on taking action. It was time to get to work.

"There are also some more properties in Harlem for sale. Some nice brownstones for about the same price. I think you should get them, also."

"I think so too. Let's do it. I have about one million in cash to invest for now. So put in all paperwork."

Following her meeting with Ms. Elma, Lady went home. Sitting in her couch, she thought about her mother. The Jamaicans had taken her out and, without a doubt in her mind, she had to get some revenge. Her mother would not just die in vain. Repercussions were necessary. She would deal with things accordingly.

Drac called, taking her out of her thoughts.

"What's up, babe?" she answered.

"The big boys got Mark," he said.

"Oh yea? I never heard about that."

Usually, Lady got all information pertaining to the happenings in the streets. She was surprised she hadn't heard Mark got nabbed by the FEDS.

"Yeah, they caught him down in Florida. I just got word from one of my cousins. Watch yourself out there. He might be talking."

"You know I'm on point."

"Also, keep an eye out on the big one. He's out there wilding."

Lady already knew who Drac was talking about. *Big Bear.*

"Understood," she said.

"Do what you gotta do to protect yourself."

"I will."

Hanging up with Drac, Lady placed a call to Bert.

"What's good, boss lady?" answered Bert.

"Time for some action. We're gonna meet up tonight to discuss some things."

"Say no more, b."

Chapter 12

Mark was bailed out in no time. His attorney automatically found holes in his case, presented it to the judge presiding over the case, and got him a half-million-dollar bail-out package. Making it back to New York, he set plans in motion to bring it to Big Bear.

It was time to take out the big man.

This was long overdue.

"That nigga killed your moms?" Mark asked Brick, the two sitting inside a Harlem ballpark.

"I just buried her yesterday," said Brick, his eyes red from crying for days. "I'm a kill that motherfucker, b."

Connecting with his cousin, Mark shared the same sentiments as Brick. They both aspired to take over the family.

Brick was the son of Big Bear's cousin, whom the latter killed in cold blood. The gruesome killing made headlines everywhere. A hole the size of a golf ball was sent through the woman's face, giving her a closed casket burial. All sorts of woman organizations came out to protest the killing, demanding that the police find the murderer right away.

"I'm really sorry about your loss, family," Mark consoled Brick. "That faggot set rules that women is off limits, and then turns around and kills a woman. *A DuPont woman at that*. He gotta die, man."

"Listen, man, I'm going for Cheryl," said Brick. "It's an eye for an eye."

"I'm with you on that. That bitch is not off-limits."

"She was. But now that Big Bear took it to the level he had, I'm gonna do the same."

Mark was glad to have Brick on his side. The man had lots of troops in Harlem and was known to not play any games. He was a significant force in the DuPont family, a serious soldier. And what made things even better, they both had the same vision. When Mark was released from the FEDS, Brick reached out. At first, he was hesitant to connect with Brick, thinking that maybe he was sent to lure him in to Big Bear. But when hearing of the incident in Rucker Park, in which he took out Shooter Sean and attempted to kill Lady, coupled with what Big Bear had done to his mother, Mark decided to take the chance of meeting up with him.

"You kind of started all this non-sense," said Brick. "But I'm not mad at you. The family needed a change, and I respect that you stepped up to the plate to make that change."

"Listen, family, Big Bear has been running the show for way too long. He's always been disrespectful to us, treating us as peons, even though we're family. I couldn't take it anymore. I hate the way he dealt with my father. And his sons…" Mark shook his head in disgust. "…those two were a problem, man."

"I fucked with Drac, but I never really liked Kevin. He killed one of my friends some years ago and I never got over that."

"Well, I never really liked both of them niggas," said Mark with conviction. "Anyway, let's get to work. I like that idea of taking out Cheryl."

"Let's do this."

After meeting up with Brick, Mark shot to the Bronx. Since the war kicked off, his drug dens had slowed up. People were scared to come outside to cop, including the crackheads. The Young Gunners had implanted fear in everyone with brazen drive-by and walkup shootings. Shooter Sean really laid it down during his time, Mark had to admit. The younger man was not normal when it came to the street shit. But with him out the way, maybe he could get things back up and running on his block.

"I need the spots back jumping," he said to some of his troops inside a building on 183rd. "Shit gotta get back to how it was. We gotta get back to the money."

Mark's soldiers listened as he spoke. One boy's attention, however, seemed to be elsewhere, causing Mark to check him.

"You don't hear me talking to you, nigga?" he barked.

Looking around at everyone present then back to Mark, the boy stared for a few seconds before speaking.

"I lost two of my brothers fucking with you. By the hands of Harlem niggas. Not only that, but Harlem niggas led by a bitch. I can't fuck with you like that," he said.

Stuck for a few seconds, Mark knew he had better react. If he didn't, everyone present would think he was soft. He could not let the boy get away with his disrespect. Moving for the boy, he was surprised when one man got in the way.

"Nah, Mark," spoke up Carl, a somewhat underboss in Mark's Bronx operation. "I can't let you do that. Shorty's right."

Mark gave Carl a questioning look. He could not believe Carl was stepping up for the boy. During their come up, such a move made by anyone, they would have pulverized the individual. So he was stuck as to why Carl was taking a stand against him.

"What you mean, Carl?"

"What I mean is that shorty's right. We lost a lot of niggas during this war over your family. We ain't DuPont's, and don't want to be DuPont's. *This is what's the word, 183rd over here.* We not fighting your family war no more. You could go do that shit in Harlem. We'll accept our losses."

Stunned, Mark looked around at his troops. All wore defensive faces as if they were on Carl's side and would attack him if they had to. He felt naked, completely vulnerable. At a loss to his own people. If he didn't have the Bronx on his side in the ongoing war, what would he do? He couldn't fight Big Bear by himself.

Nonetheless, he had to get out of his current situation. It seemed like his troops were on the verge of attacking him, so he had to get ghost before he ended up dead.

"I understand where y'all coming from, man," he said, accepting defeat. Though it was hard to do such a thing, he had no choice.

"Check it, Mark, I know you, nigga," said Carl. "Been knowing you for years, and I know how you move. So be careful with your sneak plays. I'm a let you leave, but, please, don't show your face out here again."

Mark felt like his stomach dropped to the floor with Carl's words. He was completely defeated. His right-hand man, Carl, had banned him from his block. It didn't matter that he'd put in so much work for 183rd, killed in the name of the block on countless occasions, brought riches to the neighborhood, stood up against *everyone* for the block, he was now ousted from his position of top man. Completely embarrassed, he found it hard to turn and walk out the building.

He just stared at Carl.

"What you waiting on, nigga?" Carl asked in a defensive tone. "Leave the block!"

"Come on, Carl, you gonna do me like that?" Mark asked, still surprised at what was taking place.

"Listen, man, get up outta here before it gets ugly, nigga. We not DuPont's over here. Go to Harlem with that shit. Y'all niggas had the block long enough. We don't want y'all over here no more. We'll accept our losses. But we're not taking anymore."

"But you my nigga, man."

A boy out the group quickly moved to Mark, punching him dead in the face.

Instinctively, Mark swung back at the boy. However, his punch was weaved. The boy tossed a barrage more blows, all colliding with Mark's face, flooring him. He tried getting up but was kicked in the face, sent back to the floor.

"Enough!" Spoke up Carl, commanding the boy to stop.

From the floor, Mark looked up at Carl and the rest. He barely could see out of one eye. It felt like it was shut, closed. His face ached from all the punches the younger boy hit him with.

"Get up and leave," Carl warned again. "Next time I won't stop him from beating on you."

Gathering up himself, Mark got up. Wobbling a bit, he looked at Carl once more before leaving, hoping that his friend would have a change of heart. However, Carl looked back his way with a carefree expression. Putting his head down, Mark left the building.

Beyond embarrassed, Mark went to his car, getting inside. Surveying his block for the last time, memories of his childhood came to mind. Growing up on 183rd was an event. One had to have tough skin to survive on the rough Bronx block, maybe the roughest street in the borough. He fought for his reputation, eventually garnering the leading role of the strip, a feat many had died trying to accomplish. However, just like he earned it, it was taken away. The guys who were there with him on his rise to the top had now turned their backs on him. It was damn near impossible to fight them all to regain his position, so he had no choice but to vacate the scene.

Putting the car in gear, he drove off.

Chapter 13

The heat was on. Police searched for Big Bear everywhere. He was officially a wanted man. Posters with his face printed on them were up all over Harlem.

Murder was the case.

The police wanted him for three murders inside Rucker Park, none of which he committed. Brick's foolish move put him in the hot seat, leaving him on the run once again in life.

Staying in Polo Grounds was out of the question. That was the first place the police went to search for him. He left the borough for Queens, staying in a low-key pad in the Springfield section. No one knew of his whereabouts, not even Cheryl, and he liked things that way. He went outside only when he had to. Usually, that was to go and buy food items. Through a soldier, he ran the family business from his confines. Until his attorney figured things out, he decided to stay put in his cave.

Hitting the floor for some pushups, he began a set when he got a call from Cheryl.

"What's going on, babe?"

Cheryl spoke in a frantic tone. "I just got word that guys are outside waiting to do me something."

"What?" asked Big Bear. "Who?"

"Brick. Somebody just came and told me he's in the projects looking for me with a couple other guys."

"I'm on the way."

Big Bear hung up the phone, rushed to get ready, shooting out the apartment once he was through. Racing to Harlem, he made it to Polo Grounds in no time.

Police were everywhere when he reached. Yellow tape lined the playground. Someone was killed, Big Bear could tell. He parked across the street from the projects and could see a still figure on the ground. A boy from the projects passed his car and he called him over.

"What happened in there?"

"Lady and the Young Gunners came through and tore shit up," answered the boy.

"Oh yea?"

"Yep."

Taking the risk of going inside to see if Cheryl was okay, he locked up the car and got out. Keeping his head straight, he walked around one of the buildings to the back section, ignoring stares from passerby's.

"Ain't that Big Bear?" one girl asked a next as they passed.

The other girl damn near broke her neck to see Big Bear, but he'd already made it inside the building.

He got in the elevator and went upstairs.

"How did you get by all those cops?" Cheryl asked Big Bear, shocked that he showed up.

"I got my ways," said Big Bear, brushing off Cheryl. "Anyway, what happened out there?"

"I called up Lady and she came out here in a hurry. I didn't know how far away you was, so I reached out to her."

"What the fuck you call that bitch for? I told you I was on the way."

"'Bear, those guys made it to the building and were on the way up. When I called Lady, she made a quick call and had one of the Young Gunners from in the building handle those niggas."

Pissed off with Cheryl, Big Bear took a seat in a couch.

How had the family got so out of control?

Something like what occurred would not have happened prior to him going to jail, especially not with actual members of the family. It was like he lost control of what he gave birth to, *the DuPont clan*. His own family was after his life, targeting his wife, out to wipe him off the face of the earth. Never, since he structured the family, has anything like this ever happened.

Nonetheless, he was Big Bear. The giant of Harlem, as he referred to himself. There was no man in the world he would back down from. So if his family wanted to play the role of the enemy, then so be it.

He would treat them like the enemy.

"Cheryl, I told you I don't want that little bitch in family business. You was supposed to wait on me."

"I was supposed to wait to die?"

Cheryl had a point. Though Big Bear made it over in a hurry, probably Brick and his people would have gotten to her before he reached over.

"So, what happened?"

"What happened is that Lady and her people got crazy, shooting down a couple of Brick's soldiers. You see what's going on outside."

"I want you to come out to Queens with me to lay low."

"'Bear, you know I'm not leaving Polo Grounds."

"Why are you so stubborn, man?"

For years, Big Bear had been trying to get Cheryl out of Polo Grounds, but she refused to leave. Out of all the places she could have lived, she made the ultimate decision to stay put in the projects, where she felt more comfortable.

As Big Bear, Cheryl and her family was some of the first people to move to Polo Grounds. She never left the projects since moving in, even though she possessed many riches. Not even Big Bear could get her to change her mind to leave.

"This is why our son lost his life, and our next son lost his freedom. Because you want to stay here," argued Big Bear.

"Don't you dare blame that on me. I told you years ago that you can take them out the projects. *You* chose to let them stay," Cheryl argued back.

"How was I supposed to raise the boys without their mother that they loved? Why the fuck couldn't you just break out of the projects mentality?"

Cheryl began to cry.

Deep down, she knew Big Bear was right. She was stuck in a certain mental state, a state of comfort. Most of her life was spent in Polo Grounds. This was where her mother and father raised her, *where it all began*. Losing her parents to sickness took a major toll on her well-being, and mental state. She never got over the loss, and found herself, along the years, fighting to heal. However, she was unable to. Her parents were her world, key factors in her life, the main reason she stayed in the projects. Giving up her apartment would be like giving up on her parents. Or so she trained herself to think. She never got rid of their things; she kept everything neatly packed away inside the room they use to stay in. Their aura was very much still present in the apartment, and she refused go because of this, even against chastisement from Big Bear and other members of her family.

"You're rich," they would say.

But it didn't matter about riches. Clearly, she could have been living like the movie stars. Her bank account could match up to any of the celebrities' making raves in the industry. It was just that she was a first-generation Polo Grounds Towers resident that truly did not want to leave the projects, which, in her mind, would be like leaving her parents behind. *I can't do that.*

"I don't really care about that crying shit!" roared Big Bear. "Our children needed their mother, and I wasn't just gonna take them from you. You had to be there to raise them."

"Please, 'Bear, stop it!" cried Cheryl. "You're right! Okay? You're right!"

She ran off to her room.

One thing about Big Bear, he didn't care about tears. He was a hardcore fellow that was hard to move. *Emotions are for bitches*, was his view on things.

A man had to be man. Because of the love and respect he had for Cheryl, he never enforced certain things on her like he did with his other women. Which turned out to be a huge mistake, that cost him his sons to streets. If they were going to grow up in the projects, he needed them to be tough. Regardless of who their father was, they had to be able to stand up for themselves. That was mandatory in his book. Submitting to Cheryl's stubbornness, he began to toughen up his boys, making them the men they turned out to be.

Aggravated, Big Bear left the apartment, heading downstairs. There were still police everywhere, searching the atmosphere for evidence. He and an officer caught eye contact on his way to his car. Quickly turning away, he made it inside his ride, starting it and driving off right away.

It was too late, though.

He was already spotted.

As he drove off, he saw the officer on a walkie-talkie, probably identifying his car to his colleagues, while pointing at him to his co-workers on the scene. The officers began to run toward their cars, obviously to pursue him. Pressing down on the gas, the car shot up the street, racing away. Making a quick turn on a narrow block, he lost control of the vehicle, crashing into a parked car. His head hit the steering wheel, knocking him out completely.

When Big Bear came to, he was chained to a hospital bed, surrounded by Federal agents who seemed to have been there for a while waiting for him to wake up. His body was in pain, aching all over.

"One thing about you criminals, y'all never know when to leave your original habitat alone. I knew you would return to Polo Grounds," said a red-faced agent.

Keeping silent, Big Bear allowed the agent to talk without intervening. Afterall, the agent was right. Most guys he knew usually got arrested in their neighborhood, the majority not having nowhere to go, anyway. He felt stupid, though, because he did have a place to go. And lots of money to place him anywhere on the planet.

"We found the gun in the car. We have witnesses that saw you kill those people in Rucker Park. And we are building more evidence against you for multiple more crimes," continued the agent.

If there was a witness in the Rucker Park shooting, *they were a damn lie*, thought Big Bear. However, he was not going to go back-and-forth with the agents about if he was involved or not. They would have to do their own investigative work if they wanted an answer of his involvement. Obviously, he was on his way to jail, maybe the FEDS this time, a joint he had never been to before. He doubted if he said anything that it would change something.

It is what it is.

"Let's get out of here," said one of the agents when realizing Big Bear was giving them the silent treatment.

The agents left the room, leaving Big Bear alone to his thoughts. He had to get to his attorney, was his first thoughts. Then Cheryl to make sure she had money ready just in case they offered a bail. Other than that, he would have to just sit and wait things out.

Chapter 14

When Lady got the call from Cheryl, it was a must she reacted in a haste manner. The lady's voice sounded urgent.

"Get somebody over here now!" ordered Cheryl.

It didn't matter that Big Bear had told her to fall back. Through Drac, she and Cheryl had built a tight relationship and there was no way she would leave the woman out to fry. Getting on the phone with Bert, she demanded that he get on the scene of Polo Grounds, *asap!*

Cheryl needed help.

Rushing to the scene herself, Lady came too late. The Young Gunners had already tore shit up, sending Brick and his crew running up outta the projects. Some weren't so lucky to make it out, though. A few bodies lied on the pavement, dead from bullet wounds. Rushing up to Cheryl, Lady was happy to see that Brick had not made it up to her.

"Are you okay?" she'd asked Cheryl.

"Yes," replied Cheryl.

"How did you know they were coming?"

"A friend of mine rushed up to my apartment and told me Brick and some men were outside asking about my whereabouts. They went as far as saying they're gonna kill me when they catch me for what Big Bear had done to Brick's mother."

Glad to have been able to help Cheryl, Lady vacated the projects before the police showed up. On the way out, she ran into Bert, whom she had assigned the position of new leader of the Young Gunners. She and the boy, who was younger than her, had built a bond since Shooter Sean's death. Bert was hellbent on revenge for what happened to Shooter Sean, just as she was, but because of the delicate situation with Big Bear, she told him to hold standfast until Drac said different.

"We put in that work," Bert had said, glad to get one up on Brick. "I tried to catch that nigga, but he ran like the bitch he was."

Lady was upset Bert had not caught Brick. She wished he grounded the other man with a shot. Unfortunately, he didn't.

Brick made it to see another day.

Things were getting sticky. Members of Big Bear's family was now after him, Brick especially, whose mother was slaughtered because of something he did.

Hearing of the vicious act Big Bear committed, Lady wanted no parts of the DuPont boss. Why would he kill his own cousin? For something her son did? His coldness was puzzling. He did not have to kill the woman as he had.

Before Lady got the chance to go and see Drac to inform him about the close call with his mother, she got word that Big Bear was arrested following the incident in Polo Grounds. He was captured leaving the projects. Then and there, she realized he had a little *stupid* in his blood. There was no way he was supposed to visit the projects after what happened. If anything, he was supposed to send some troops over to defend his wife. His foolish move cost him his freedom. Lady doubted he would ever see the streets again. Which meant she was back in position to hold things down for Drac. Now was time for her to get to work and destroy *all* DuPont enemies, chiefly the Jamaicans who'd killed her mother.

She got ready to go and see Drac. Shooting out the house, she made it to the jail in no time. Going through the regular process, she was let on the floor to see Drac.

"Whatever happened to that guy the time I was on the visit that was ice grilling me?" Lady asked before she forgot.

Drac made up his face like he was trying to remember who Lady was talking about.

"Mark's friend," she said when realizing Drac was stuck.

"Oh, yea," said Drac, as if a lightbulb had gone on in his head. "Some niggas got at him in here. Sent him out the facility. We never even got the chance to cross paths again."

"Okay."

"Fuck that nigga, though. How's things with you?"

Lady went into explain what she had been going through. The pain with losing her mother and everything that was going in the streets.

"My father is a stupid nigga."

Drac shook his head in shame. After receiving a reversal for a murder that he *really* committed, Big Bear was back in the can, facing a potential death sentence.

Why he couldn't just chill?

His reckless moves had, *once again*, sunk him to possibly a land of the unknown. His eagerness for complete power had stripped him of his freedom, taking him away from his family, again. There was no coming back for Big Bear, unless some sort of miracle happened. If not, his career in the streets was over.

Lady held her opinions to herself. Disrespecting Big Bear out loud had always been an act of transgression that could cost one their life, so she kept her cool, sticking to the rules, even though she knew she couldn't really get in trouble for that right about now.

"That motherfucker never even came to see me before he got himself trapped off again," vented Drac. "Every time I called the crib, I never could get to him. He just went out there and forgot about everything and got himself caught up again. Fucking dick head."

The anger in Drac's voice resonated to Lady. She felt his pain. He was upset with his father for sure reasons. In her eyes, Big Bear got what he deserved. He was a woman killing, power hungry, savage that should be buried beneath someone's prison. She would never help him out in his situation, even if Drac demanded this of her.

Blowing out a loud breath, Drac shook his head before changing course in the conversation.

"But what I did find out was that he had nothing to do with Shooter Sean's death. That, at least, made me feel a little better. Brick took the initiative himself to do that," he said.

Just as Drac, Lady had heard the same thing. Big Bear was not involved with what had taken place in Rucker Park. He was actually against Brick's move. So much that he went to kill Brick but was almost killed himself. Hence, bringing forth the death of Brick's mother. Though Lady understood Big Bear's reason for killing Brick's mother, she still didn't believe he should have taken things that far. He should have just continued to hunt Brick, killing the man when he caught him.

"I was a bit glad, also, to hear that he had nothing to do with Shooter Sean's death, but that shit he did to Brick's mother…" Lady shook her head. "…that was foul, b."

"I agree with you a hundred percent on that. That move right there completely split the family even more."

Drac got word that family members were against Big Bear's move. This was not the first time he harmed a family member, but the first time he did it for no strong reason. Brick's mother was not supposed to be brought in the conflict. She had nothing to do with what was going on.

Drac continued, "A lot of people not fucking with my pops behind that move. He went too far with that move."

"So what's the next move?"

Staring off into the busy visiting room, Drac thought about Lady's question.

What is the next move?

During all his years, he never experienced this division in the family. Everyone was united, following the directions of Big Bear and his brothers. But now, with the younger generation of DuPont's at war, the family's future stood in limbo. It wasn't guaranteed that things could get back together. Major blood was spilled during the internal conflict, people were killed. The situation was beyond sticky, and maybe was unrepairable.

"Honestly," started Drac, coming back from his daze, "I don't know."

He really didn't.

"Well, I'm letting you know from now that I'm sicking the dogs on those Jamaicans who killed my mother," said Lady in a serious tone of voice.

Drac couldn't dispute Lady's plan. Partially, he felt at blame for her mother's death. Had he not got her in his family's mess, Lady's mother would more than likely still be around. But she perished in the nasty war going on in Harlem, igniting a fire within Lady. As he stared across the visit room table at her eyes, he could tell Lady was not the same girl he *officially* met the day in the elevator. Her eyes showed hurt, alertness, the power to achieve. She was a changed woman, visibly on a mission.

"Lady, the family is in your hands now. You've proved that you can run this shit on your own. Do what you have to do. You have the resources for everything you need. Utilize them to the best of your ability. I got your back a thousand percent. That's without a doubt. You saved my mother's life, so I got you for life," he explained.

Drac's words meant everything to Lady. She truly loved and cared for him and would never leave his side. As long as she was around, she would fight for his freedom and well-being.

Making it back to Queens after the visit with Drac, Lady set her plans in motion. Calling a dinner meeting with Bert and the Young Gunners, coupled with a few other people she'd connected with, it was time to get to work as the official leader of the DuPont's.

Chapter 15

Mark met up with his brother, Bill, on a side block in Harlem. He wanted to explain to him what occurred in the Bronx, among other things. He also wanted to open up about things that he'd been keeping a secret for some time now, things that had been eating away at his brain.

"Bro, shit just been crazy out here, man. The whole crew flipped on me in the BX. This war with the family got my head in the clouds. It's just too much," Mark said, shaking his head.

Sitting quiet in the passenger seat of Mark's ride, Bill stared out at passing cars.

Mark continued, "I need for you to take over what I have going on. I'm falling back."

Prior to coming to meet with Bill, Mark had made up his mind to give the streets a break. The pressure was *too* thick. He couldn't manage. Brick would have to fight the battle himself. His plan was to hand over his drug operation to his brother as he focused on his legitimate businesses.

Bill remained quiet.

"So you ready to take this thing over?" Mark asked, wondering why Bill was so quiet.

As Bill looked straight ahead at the road, a tear fell from his eye. Slowly, he turned to face Mark.

He asked, "Take this thing over?" his face distorting into that of anger.

Mark was taken aback by Bill's transformation.

What the fuck?

"Take this thing over?" Bill repeated. "The cat is out the hat, Mark. I know you killed dad. I been knew. But because I love you so much, I tried my best to be loyal and down."

"I don't know what you're talking 'bout?" Mark said right away.

"Yes, you do, nigga!"

"Watch your fucking tone with me!"

Bill had never come at Mark in this manner; it was surprising. As the older brother, he had heavy influence over Bill, the latter usually did what he said to do. However, something was going on now that he could not understand.

"No, nigga, you watch your tone! Because of your greed, you fucked shit up in the family. Now look what's going on, everybody's at war. All because you want to be the head of things. And now you got the nerve to talk about you want to back out now. *Hell no, nigga!* You ain't backing out of shit. You're gonna fight this war you started."

Mark slammed an elbow into Bill's mouth, rocking his head. Jumping across his seat, he began to choke out his brother, who fought back, swinging wild blows. The car rattled as the two fought. Both threw haymakers, punching each other all over. The bout went on-and-on until, finally, Mark took out a gun and fired a shot, hitting Bill in the stomach.

The bullet took the fight out of Bill. He sat, wide-eyed, in his seat, in complete shock, staring at Mark.

Angry, Mark looked back at Bill with a carefree expression. In a zone, he did not care that he shot Bill. His brother should have known better than to try and fight him.

Bill's eyes went from wide to slowly closing as his life force began its descent out of his body.

Coming to his senses, Mark grabbed a hold of Bill's shirt collar and began to shake him.

"Stay up, nigga!" he shouted while shaking his brother. "Stay up, nigga!"

Deep down, he knew better.

Bill was a goner.

He'd experienced the same scenario many times in the past. He could tell when someone was dead.

"Damn, nigga! Why the fuck you made me do this to you?!"

Bill was unresponsive. He'd passed away.

Falling back in his seat, Mark started to cry. Emotions ran through him, rattling his mind. Memories of his brother's childhood days flooded his mind. They grew up together in the Bronx, in the same household. Because of their father's busy schedule, they practically were raised by their mother. Though they had a well-off life, much better than neighborhood counterparts, they were still confined to one of the roughest sections of the city. Mark defended his brother anytime a conflict arose in the streets, but, really, he didn't have to. Bill was a warrior, a true to life DuPont, down for whatever. The respect he had for Mark was almost unreal. Mark meant the world the Bill. He would do whatever for his older brother.

Looking over at Bill, Mark cried more as he watched his brother leaned over in the seat.

"Why you had to come at me like that, man?" he said.

Bill was long gone, though. Dead to the world.

Left with no other option, Mark had to dispose of the body.

Fixing Bill upright in his seat, Mark strapped his body with the seatbelt to keep him from leaning forward. Driving through Harlem, he kept looking over at Bill during the drive. Tears poured from his eyes every time. He was past hurt. Pushing through, he ended the journey on Edgecombe Avenue. He'd made a vow to never fuck with Donovan again, but now was left without a choice. His crew had flipped, along with his family, and even his brother. Donovan was maybe the only person he could count on now. Parking the vehicle, he got out the car and went into the building the Jamaicans usually hung out in.

"Is Donovan around?" he asked a young Jamaican man.

"Who wants to know?" the man asked in his thick accent.

"Mark."

Screwing Mark from head-to-toe before walking off deeper inside the building, the man came back with Donovan and a few other men in tow, all of whom watched Mark with hawk eyes.

Donovan wore a smirk as he looked at Mark, whom he had not seen nor heard from in a while.

"Long time no hear," he started. "I called you a few times and you ignored my calls."

Donovan was right. Mark had been ducking him ever since they raped and killed Lady's mother. He wanted no parts of the act, so he stayed away.

"I was lying low, Donovan. You know how we do. I was just trying to make things cool off a bit. That's all," he explained.

Wearing his usual serious gaze, Donovan shook his head.

"So, what's up? What can I do for you?"

Looking from his men to Donovan, he gave a head gesture indicating that he wanted to speak with him alone out the earshot of everyone.

"Everybody go back to the back," Donovan instructed, understanding that Mark wanted to speak with him alone.

Donovan's men quickly walked off.

"What's going on?" Donovan asked.

Mark explained what occurred with his brother. "I need your help, man," he said.

Donovan gave Mark the evil eye. He looked like he was on the verge of attacking Mark.

"You're really bright, nigga," he spat. "My sister got killed because of *you*. You disappeared, never even showed up to pay respects at her funeral, and now you want *me* to help you get rid of your little brother's body? Nigga, you stupid? I should shoot you in your pussy."

Donovan's men came out from the back when hearing their bosses' venomous words. All approached, staring Mark down.

Nervous, Mark wore a weary expression, hoping that Donovan didn't set his men on him.

"I'm sorry, man," was all he could say.

Donovan had all rights to feel how he felt. After all, he'd helped Mark out many times in the past, put his soldiers on the line. Lost many of his people because of assisting Mark to take over his family. He had all rights to kill Mark, but Mark hoped he didn't make such a move.

"Let me tell you something," started Donovan. "You better leave this building and never come back. I'm gonna give you the chance to do this just once. Next time I see you, I'm a put a bullet through you."

Quickly backtracking out the building, Mark broke into a sprint once outside, racing for his car. If Donovan changed his mind, Mark would easily be murdered, and he was not ready to die.

He'd lost his last allegiance in the streets with Donovan. He was now all alone in the cold world of New York City.

Back in his ride, he noticed his brother's body had tilted a little bit. Bill's head now rested on the passenger side window. Fixing his head as straight as it would go, Mark saw that blood soaked the feet area in the ride. Bill's wound was leaking profusely. Also, a foul stench now reeked in the air. Mark was familiar with the smell.

He shitted himself.

Now that he was on his own, completely, he had to figure out where he could dump Bill's body. He had to get him out the car before someone noticed.

Pulling off, he circled the entire westside of Harlem before he found what seemed like a vacant backstreet. Reversing the ride to the far back end of the street, next to a couple garbage dumpsters, he parked and got out the car. Searching the block for any movement, he walked around to Bill's side when seeing the coast was clear. Opening the door, he struggled to take Bill out. His brother had always been on the hefty side. Pulling Bill to a hydrant on the street, he rested his body on the metal slab. Looking around once more, he went back and closed the passenger door before shooting back to his side of the car, getting inside. Once secure in the ride, he took off.

It hurt to have to dump his little brother in the streets like a dog, but what was he to do? It's not like he could have dropped him off at a hospital. Staff there would want to know what happened, putting him on the spot. Such a move would have surely landed him in prison.

Wiping tears from his eyes, he felt alone in the world. He no longer had anyone to turn to. The streets had gotten the best of him. If he didn't move right, the dogs would surely eat his food. Headed for his lay low spot in Brooklyn, he contemplated his next move.

Part 2

Chapter 16

Perched on the head of his apartment building's steps, Brick observed 119th Street, keeping a close eye on every car that passed on the block. This was nothing new, he'd always been on the lookout when outside. Enemy forces were always gunning for the street's headliners.

Through his mother, Brick was born into the DuPont family. Though his father was a Smith, he married his mother and took on the DuPont last name, also. Harlem was ruled by the DuPont's and most people yearned to be a part of the notorious clan. Luckily, Brick came in naturally, birthed by a first cousin of Big Bear.

He wore his family last name like a badge of honor, taking a stand against anyone who dared challenge his clan's repute. His hulky size, mean scowl, and serious demeanor put him at an advantage to the flock outside. He was a real one! Through and through. Niggas knew better than to fuck with him.

All Brick's years of existence, his respect was through the roof for Big Bear. His older cousin was his idol, who he wanted to be like, even over his own father. Big Bear's reputation spoke for itself. When he came around, especially on 119th, niggas got low, tucked their possessions, and stayed in line. At the forefront of it all, Brick watched, staying by his cousin's side whenever he was around, praying that someone acted up so he could prove himself to the family's general.

"You're a real one," Big Bear would always say.

This made him feel special. To be called a *real one* by someone like Big Bear was a big deal. It was indescribable how Brick felt when his cousin mentioned these words.

Just as Mark, his cousin, though, he aspired to take over the family, especially after he reached in his mid-twenties. Before even Mark himself took the step forward with going for it. When Big Bear was sent away and Kevin took over,

Brick felt like his cousin wasn't built for the position of head DuPont. The two had grown together, did a lot in the streets as co-defendants, so Brick knew Kevin's levels. He was an animal as his father, but not a thinker. No leader material. His early demise came because of this he lacked. Had Kevin thought out things more precisely, he could have dismantled the Jamaicans who eventually dismantled him.

Drac, on the other hand, was different.

Brick saw something in him that he knew did not exist in Kevin. The younger DuPont had brains, style, *and the heart of a lion.* If he was not sent to jail, things would have surely been different with the family. But he was sent to jail and decided to marry a non-descript *bitch* that had no rights to go against the DuPont's, even Mark who had blatantly showed his disloyalty for the family.

When Brick learned of Drac's move, to control the family through Lady, he instantly got on the defense. Calling a meeting among his The Mob faction in Harlem, he let everyone know that they would not be taking any orders from Lady and the Young Gunners. He would allow them to do what they do in their section of Harlem, but once they crossed the line on the eastside, it would be on. So when Shooter Sean showed up on 119th, Brick stepped to him right away.

At the time, he had no intentions of making the block hot, but the way Shooter Sean reacted caused Brick to press the button, instructing his soldier to handle business. Before he got the chance to get out the way, though, Lady, from the circumference of the ride she and Shooter Sean had showed up in, shot his soldier. Quickly, he dispersed inside the building. That's when more shots went off.

After everything quelled, he went outside and found his soldier lying dead on the ground. That's when he decided to take it to Lady and the Young Gunners.

Linking up with Big Bear, Brick was invited to the Rucker Park basketball game by his older cousin. At the game, on the whim, Big Bear tapped him and instructed him to follow him over to where Lady, Shooter Sean, and the Young Gunners held court. Big Bear checked them like the gangster he was, and demanded that they leave the park, which they did. Brick had not even known Big Bear had an issue with Lady, and thought she was still a major factor in the family. This interaction proved he was wrong. Seeing that this was the case, and that it was his only shot to get at Shooter Sean from what he'd done to his soldier, Brick broke off from his group and shot the man in the head, then aimed at Lady. However, before he got the chance to shoot her, someone with Big Bear's entourage grabbed his hand, causing him to fire a wild shot that hit and killed someone else.

All hell broke loose after that.

Big Bear sent for him after the incident, but there was no way he would willingly turn himself over. His cousin would surely kill him if he did. Instead, he prepared to go to war. Lining up his troops, he waited on Big Bear.

He knew he was coming.

He always did.

When he did, it was a bang out.

Brick let Big Bear and his troops know that he meant business, that he was not running from no one. No matter who it was. Taking things overboard, as he was known to do, Big Bear killed Brick's mother for him taking a stand. Making a promise to himself, Brick vowed to hunt down and kill anyone affiliated with Big Bear, including anyone in the DuPont family.

"I don't care about that DuPont shit no more," Brick said to a shooter in tow. "That shit is a thing of the past. Them niggas passed they place when my mother was killed."

Riding on the westside of Harlem, Brick hunted anyone a part of the DuPont's. Following his mother's untimely demise, something switched in his head. He'd been a live nigga, but her death made him even livelier. For the smallest infraction, he yearned to spill blood. From here on out, the world would know he meant business.

"I'm with you on that, boss man," said Snap, a small-framed shooter a part of Brick's team.

He rode shotgun with his boss, carrying a large caliber pistol on his lap.

It was daytime out. The streets of Harlem were crowded with people, walking to-and-fro on the concrete pavements of the city. Some sort of political diplomat was in town, giving rise to a heavy traffic presence. Horns blared aloud as angry transmuters signaled their frustrations with the current gridlock in effect.

Creeping along with the short speed of the traffic, Brick kept a keen eye on the street. Hoping to catch sight of a foe. As Snap, a .9mm Browning rested on his lap, the weapon filled with bullets.

13 shots.

No doubts occupied his mind of what he would do with the strap. He would use it if he had to. When he had to. Anytime he had to. It didn't matter who was present. If a renegade DuPont, as he called the new enemy force within the family, had the nerve to stick his or her head out, Brick would blast them away. Even if the police were present. That's how real he listed the war as. It was that deep.

"Look at that nigga," Snap said, leaning forward in his seat, motioning toward a black male exiting a passageway in Polo Grounds.

They were now just outside Polo Grounds.

Observing the male Snap spotted, Brick pulled over, bringing the vehicle to a double-park stop. The last time he came to Polo Grounds, he was ambushed by the Young Gunners, who were lucky enough to strike before he made it up to Cheryl's apartment. He let it be known he was on the hunt for Cheryl, a blunder on his part, revealing his intentions to a few passerby's he knew from Polo Grounds. In turn, clearly, they sounded off the alarm, alerting the projects' protectors of his presence and intentions. A shoot-out ensued and he lost a few men.

This time around he had to practice discipline.

Don't let the emotions get the best of me.

Slither like a snake through the jungle under guise. Then strike!

Grabbing the door latch to exit the vehicle, a loud horn sounded off, startling Brick.

"What the fuck?!"

He blocked someone in with his vehicle. The person wanted to come out of the parking space.

"I should clap that motherfucker," Snap vented, startled just as Brick from the loud horn. His heart raced from the sudden shock of the noise.

"Word, b," agreed Brick.

Looking over at the car, adjacent his, he, and the person inside made eye contact.

It was a man.

Instantly, an alarm blared in his head.

Enemy!

Snap had yet to recognize his facial transformation, signaling his next move. The boy was still uptight about the loud, startling horn.

"These motherfuckers need to be more cautious of what they're doing," he spoke aloud to himself.

Getting a hold of his pistol, Brick, quickly, aimed at his passenger's side window.

Instinctively, Snap, snapping back to his senses, leaned as far back as he could.

Brick had no time to explain what was occurring. All he knew was that he had to get to the guy in the car.

Bang!

The spark of the discharged firearm lit up like a flame.

Gun powder sprinkled Snap's face, the combustion instantly burning his flesh. Screaming out in agony, he fell over the car's center console, allowing Brick to continue his rampage.

Shooting out the passenger side window, Brick's firearm barked like a hungry bulldog. However, the target ducked before any bullets hit his ride. He saw it coming and reacted fast.

Bang! Bang! Bang!

Brick continued to shoot. Even after the target slipped out his ride on the passenger side. Once again, anger came back to haunt his maneuvers. The target had gotten away. Scott free. Yet, he still fired away.

Reality eventually sunk in.

The nigga got away already, man.

There was no use in wasting bullets. He stopped shooting.

Snap was curled up like a baby, looking as if he were in a fetal position.

Brick felt bad for firing the weapon so close to his face, possibly scarring him for life. *But what was I supposed to do?* If he hadn't reacted, the other *nigga* probably would have reacted.

"You good?" he asked Snap.

Putting the car in gear, he raced off the scene before Snap got the chance to respond.

Getting up right in his seat, Snap quickly pulled down the mirrored sun visor to see his face. Small, blister type burns were everywhere. The gun powder had surely done a number on his face. He was possibly scarred for life.

"Nah, man. My shit look fucked up."

Brick took a quick glimpse at Snap's face before focusing back on the road.

"You'll be alright," he said.

"What the fuck happened back there?"

Snap wanted to know. He still did not know why Brick reacted in the manner he had.

"I saw one of the Young Gunner niggas. He was the one try'na get out the parking space. As soon as I seen who it was, I let it fly."

"As you should."

Snap felt a little better to know his face was not messed up in vain. It was for an essential reason. One he respected.

Making it back on the eastside in one piece, Brick dropped Snap home and went about his business. He would be back to Polo Grounds the following evening, he promised himself.

Chapter 17

Visiting Los Angeles for the first time, Lady loved the scenery. Nice weather; palm trees; super clean environment, far from what she was used to in New York; warm welcoming people. What a big difference in comparison to her hometown. Right away, she fell in love with the vibe of LA.

Ms. Elma had someone pick her up. *Paul.* An elderly Latino man. A realtor from Los Angeles, who would be showing her available properties for sale.

Lady was getting deeper-and-deeper into the real estate game. Her first few purchases opened her eyes to the lucrative market. *Millionaires are made through real estate,* were Ms. Elma's *constant* slogan. *You can't lose in this game if you're consistent and disciplined,* she said.

The more Lady studied the game, the more she realized Ms. Elma was right. Thus, she went headfirst, *full-fledged,* into the game.

Lady spoke to Paul.

"I love the environment out here."

"Yes. Los Angeles is a very beautiful place."

"Much more cleaner than New York."

Lady made up her face after this remark. The filthy state of her city played like a reel in her mind. Sewer rats: garbage filled streets; pollution filled air. The list went on-and-on. New York's condition, well, at least, the condition of Harlem needed to be addressed by some sort of government official. *Expediently.*

"I completely understand where you're coming from. I've lived in New York for many years of my life," Paul mentioned.

"Oh, yea? What parts?"

"Spanish Harlem."

Familiar with the environment, Lady pressed on.

"Where out there?"

"Carver Houses."

"Okay. You're from the projects?"

"Yes."

Paul stopped at a light.

An old school, fire red Cadillac pulled up alongside their ride. Four men inside, sporting red bandannas that covered the bottom portion of their faces, with baseball caps of the same hue, eyed Lady, and Paul.

Paul kept his head straight, avoiding eye contact with the men.

That New Yok fire within Lady forced her to return the gesture. In return, she eyed the men.

Why're they wearing all that red?

One of the men, the driver, pulled the bandanna from his face, cracked a smirk, and then skidded off once the light turned green.

Paul continued to drive.

"What the hell is wrong with those guys?" Lady wanted to know.

"Those are the Bloods."

The Bloods?

"What do you mean? Is that some sort of clique or something?"

"It's a gang that wears the color *red* to identify themselves. They fight with the Crips gang, who wears the color *blue*."

Lady laughed.

"That sounds mad corny, b."

"That's the lifestyle in California. Gangs run the streets. Unlike New York, where drug crews control the blocks."

Paul's history lesson revealed some important information. *Don't be fooled by the palm trees.* Lady had to be alert. As New York, it was clear California had its own culture...*in the streets.*

Drug gangs ran the Big Apple.

Color gangs ran Los Angeles.

As much as it seemed corny, the eyes of the Bloods she happened to cross paths with showed a seriousness she was all too familiar with. Had they accepted her eye-fight challenge, the car would have easily been Swiss-cheesed with bullets, with her and Paul inside.

From here on out, she had to proceed with caution.

"We're we headed to?"

"Ms. Elma instructed that I bring you to one of her special homes."

Lady raised an eyebrow.

Special home?

Deciding not to question Paul any further, she rested back in her seat and continued to enjoy the ride.

Close to forty-five minutes later, the car entered a gated community off Melrose Avenue in Los Angeles. State-of-the art homes bedecked the property. Expensive, foreign vehicles aligned driveways. Manicured lawns showed every sign of consistent attention. The atmosphere was *serene*. Free of distractions, noise.

Lady was in love.

"This is where Ms. Elma's home is?"

"Yep." Paul pulled into a driveway. "Right here."

The brick structure home was huge. *Almost like a palace.* Well kept, as the rest of properties she passed on the way to Ms. Elma's, the place might have had the other homes beat in size. The price tag on the property had to be within the eight-figure range. *Without a doubt.* Lady was awestruck by the property's exterior, alone. *What would inside look like*, she wondered.

Paul said, "Let's go inside."

Anticipation filled Lady as she exited the car. Excitement engrossed her thoughts. She couldn't wait to see inside Ms. Elma's castle.

"I could only imagine what inside looks like."

Paul smiled.

"You'll love it here. I can bet anything on that."

It was time to see if Paul was busting her chops.

Entering the *palace,* the name she'd christened the place, right away she was awestruck. *Oh my God!* The beauty of inside, surprisingly, surpassed that of outside. Decked out with antique furniture, *all* gold in hue, the pad resembled something out of a movie. Nothing Lady had *ever* seen before. Medieval paintings decorated gold walls, rose gold marble floor tiles made up the inside pavement. The place was clean! *Squeaky clean!* A blooming rose aroma floated through the air. Jazz music, on low tempo, played from surround sound. It felt like heaven on earth.

"Well," smiled Paul, noticing the atmosphere had captivated Lady, "make yourself comfortable. This will be your home for the next week or so."

Kicking off her shoes, Lady went over to a comfy looking couch, falling on top the expensive furniture. Paul needed not to tell her anymore. If this was to be home for the next week or so, she was sold on the idea.

Paul continued, "There's food in the kitchen. Make yourself something to eat. I'll be by later to pick up you up so that we can start property hunting."

"Okay."

Paul departed the house, leaving Lady alone. Instantly, she began to explore. Room after room. A backyard area. A basement level with a large as life swimming pool. Making way to a second-floor level, she found a room she instantly fell in love with. *This where I'm sleeping.* Jumping on a king-sized bed like a child, she rolled from side-to-side, enjoying the comfort of the huge mattress. Pausing a bit, she looked up at a glass ceiling, admiring her reflection in the mirror. Pinching her hand, she waited to wake from a dream. Squeezing harder, for some strange reason, she could not wake up. Or was it that it *wasn't* all a dream?

Of course it's not.

Reality settled in. Lady had really made it out the hood. A feat many had not accomplished. No matter how hard they tried. Who would have thought she would be rolling around on a bed in zip code 90210? *Melrose.* Only if her mother could be here to experience the feel of *escape*.

Yeah, they'd taken the giant step to get out of Harlem, making Queens their new home. But it was not the actual move out the borough she was talking about, *it was the mental escape.* Her mother couldn't escape the mentality of many from Harlem. Which led to an early departure from earth.

Shaking her from side-to-side, Lady did not want to think about that. It was all about the revel in the moment. Enjoying the present atmosphere. Leaving certain thoughts in the back of her brain.

Taking a quick shower in a luxurious bathroom, she put on some clothes and went down to the living room. She had to call out east to check in on the status of things.

"Boss lady, I'm lucky to even be speaking to you right now," said Bert.

"Why? What happened?"

Bert let out a whistle.

"Man, listen, shit got crazy out here. I was in my car parked, then, *boom,* out of nowhere, Brick pulls up next to me. I didn't know it was him at first, but when I did realize, it was too late. The nigga opened fire on me, damn near shooting his man sitting next to him in his car."

"You guys gotta be careful out there. You see, that niggas in the neighborhood looking to hurt somebody."

"I was saying the same thing. That was no coincidence that he just so happened to be in the hood. He was out there hunting."

"So you know what you gotta do. Handle your business."

"I know that's right, b."

"Other than that, any new news in the streets?"

"Oh shit! There is. I just got word about the nigga that killed your mother."

Lady was all ears. This had always been news she yearned to hear. It was a fact the Jamaicans murdered her mother, raping her during the course of their savagery, but she was not privy to the actual culprits behind the attack. Now that she had intel of who it was, she would pay *whatever* to have them skinned alive.

"*The nigga?* It was only one person?"

"Well, it's the boss of them niggas. They call him Donovan. That's who Mark was really clicked up with."

"And how do you know this?"

"I'm fucking this Jamaican bitch from over there. She gave me the full run down on everything."

Lady raised a brow. "You sure you could trust that bitch?"

"Nope. But I'm on extra point when I'm with her."

"What else she told you? She gave any info on where we could find this Donovan nigga at?"

"Got all that info, boss lady. It's all on you to press the button."

"I'll let you know. In the meantime, handle that nigga Brick."

Lady needed some time to think and planned on doing just that while in Los Angeles. New York problems would have to wait 'til later. It was time to see what California had to offer.

Chapter 18

Cruising the streets of Los Angeles, Mark found it difficult to get attuned with the city. He'd been to California many times in the past, but only for business purposes. Even on those occasions, he found himself homesick. An eagerness of returning to New York always occupied his mind then. And it was no different now. Only difference now was that he could not go back to New York. He was a wanted man there. A major manhunt for his capture was in effect there. So he had to get out of dodge or face the prospect of being locked down for the remainder of his days on earth.

Mark sucked his teeth as he maneuvered along Florence Avenue on the westside of LA. Headed for a store on closeby Normandie Avenue. The gang infested neighborhood worked his nerves. Never in life he had to be cautious of what he wore, but in Los Angeles it was different. Either you were on the red or blue side, among other color barriers in the wild, wild west. Thus, he kept things neutral, sporting black most of the time.

The trod to the store, as usual, was eventful. Two crack addicts, a woman and man, made a scene in the streets, arguing over drugs.

"You went in my shit while I was sleep and took my shit, bitch!" the man blurted out.

"No I didn't, motherfucker!" argued the woman in her defense.

There was no escaping the tongue bout.

The couple shouted for everyone to hear.

Keeping his focus ahead, Mark avoided eye contact with the arguers.

He didn't know how much longer he could stay in Los Angeles before he cracked and headed back out east. California's energy did not coincide with his spirit. The only reason he chose the state as a place of refuge was because he could not go back to Florida, where he really wanted to be. The court case there was still open, he'd already pulled a ginger-bread-man there. If he showed face in the sunshine state and was somehow pulled over for the smallest of traffic infraction, he would be a goner. Sent off to a penitentiary somewhere in west bubba fuck. *Can't have that.* So he chose the only other place he was semi-familiar with, spent lots of time in, *California*. And now he was doomed to his decision.

As he continued the journey to the store, an old-school Coupe Deville pulled up alongside him as he walked. A man in the backseat of the ride, a blue bandanna covering the bottom portion of his face, rolled down the back window and came halfway out with a shotgun, *aimed his way*.

What the fuck?!

Following his first instinct, Mark raised his hands in the air as if to indicate he was not resisting. Whatever the men wanted they could have. He had no wins in the situation and accepted this.

"Where you from, cuz?" the shotgun toting man asked.

Mark answered right away, "New York."

"I told you that nigga not from out here, cuz," voiced someone inside the car. "Let's get outta here."

Mark could not see who made the statement but was thankful for whomever it was. Obviously, the men were gang bangers, out hunting for enemies. His neighborhood of refuge was home to the Eight Trey Gangster Crips, a notorious gang who had lots of enemies. This was not the first time he'd been approached about his affiliation in the neighborhood. Luckily, he was given a pass. *Once again.*

When the bangers rode off, Mark decided to head back to his pad, a one room, temporary shack. A past business partner allowed him to stay there until he figured things out. He didn't know things would be this *crazy*, though. It was time to move on.

I can't stay out here any longer.

Inside his room, he made a call to someone he knew, a woman named Jackie.

"I need another place to stay. It's too crazy out here. These gang bangers keep running down on me, checking to see if I'm one of their enemies."

"Where you staying at?"

"The eighties."

"What the hell? Come on, Mark, someone of your caliber shouldn't be staying in those types of environments. Why would you come to LA to be in the ghetto."

"At first, I didn't know it was the ghetto. Cali' ghettoes is set up different from New York's own. We got big, nasty buildings that'll make a nigga know right away they in the ghetto. Out here, though, got residential ghettoes. I thought I was in a cool area until a I heard gunshots going off every night."

"You should have reached out to me, first. Whoever set you up with that place must not like you."

It wasn't that. But Mark did not want to reveal his hand, spilling the beans that he was on the run. The business partner who gave him the place to stay was actually a trustworthy individual who he had made lots of moves with in the past. He asked for a modest setting, which got him home to the Eight Trey Gangster Crips. He could have gotten a place in Hollywood Hills. But didn't want that. For some reason, he felt like the police would be able to find him in affluent neighborhoods quicker. Rich neighbors might see him on a morning run and alert the police about their strange new neighbor. In the hood was different. People usually minded their business there.

He ignored Jackie's disparaging remark about his business partner.

"Anyway, set me up with a spot. Somewhere nice."

"I got you. Coming your way now."

Mark began to pack the little things he had. He didn't travel with much, settling upon buying clothes when reaching California. During his time in LA, he made a few mall trips, picked up some items, mainly sweatsuits, and cosmetics. He surely missed wearing his suits, a style he picked up from his old man during adolescent years. It was nothing like sporting a three-piece-suit with some 'gator shoes.

Nothing like it.

Nonetheless, keeping a low profile required him to dress-down. His usual style of dressing would only put the spotlight on him. Something he did not want.

Jackie showed up to his house in a new, black Range Rover. Hopping out the ride, the sexy woman caught the attention of a few persons out on the street. Dressed to nines in a form-fitting Gucci outfit, her figure blasted through the garments. She was *beyond* shapely, possessing a somewhat Coca-Cola bottle shape. From Armenian descent, her beautiful features were magnifying to the eye. Almost hypnotic. She carried herself with the grace of a boss. *Confident.*

Locking up the house, Mark, carrying a duffel bag, went over to Jackie, giving her a hug with his free hand.

He said, "Looking good as usual."

"Thanks."

Popping the trunk of her truck, she took Mark's bag, placing it inside.

Mark hopped in the ride.

So did Jackie.

"I'm a bring you to a nice pad I got."

"Bring me anywhere except here." Mark pointed out the window at the neighborhood.

Jackie laughed.

"I could bet you want to leave this place. I used to do business down here with the Crips. It's pretty rough down these parts."

"I can't count the shoot-outs I've heard since being down here for such a short amount of time. These niggas are *crazy*."

Driving through the Los Angeles streets, Mark couldn't get his mind off New York. *Home.* There was no place in the world like the Big Apple. No California. *No nowhere.* The palm trees, nice weather in Cali' was a plus, but Mark would take a blistering, freezing day in his city over *any day* in California in a New York minute.

"You're quiet over there," said Jackie, caught up in the normal LA traffic.

"Just thinking."

"So what's your plans over here? You out here to cop?"

"Nah. Not this time around."

Mark met Jackie through an acquaintance years before. She was heavy in the drug game, connected to some big players. Once his supplier, they eventually mixed the business with pleasure, becoming romantically involved. Things then took a turn for the worst, at least in Mark's eyes.

Jackie fell in love and began to commit acts he disagreed with. Like calling his phone every few minutes, *literally*, threatening to have something done to him if he didn't be with her, crying like a baby all the time, among other things. *It was too much.* Mark shut her down for a while, giving her *extra* space to get her emotions in check. Eventually, they spoke again, put their differences aside and rekindled their business relationship.

"Something's wrong, I could tell. Your whole energy is off," Jackie mentioned.

You're right. But I'm not gonna tell you what it is.

"Nah, man. I'm cool. Just needed to give New York a break for a few. Shit is kind of crazy out there."

"I hear that."

Pulling into a gated community off Melrose Avenue, Jackie drove to a large house she owned in the complex.

"You still got your place here?" Mark asked.

"I'm not giving this up. You crazy?" she laughed.

Mark had money. Lots of it. Enough to fill, maybe, a huge house. But his cash was *baby money* when compared to Jackie's fortune. She came from a family of drug lords who would make the DuPont's look like a joke. Actually, her family supplied many of the DuPont's out east, those involved in the drug trade. Jackie had money that could, possibly, *easily*, last three lifetimes.

He smiled at Jackie's comment.

"Anyway, you can have the house all to yourself. I stay with my man just down the block. If you need anything, just give me a call."

Mark responded, "No problem."

He wondered if Jackie was trying to get him jealous by mentioning she had a man. If that was the case, he didn't want to burst her bubble by replying *I don't give a fuck.* It was better for him that she was involved. That kept the pressure of her possessive ways off him.

Jackie let him in the house, and he got right to getting himself comfortable.

Chapter 19

Palming the grip handle of a .9mm Ruger, filled with an extended clip that held thirty-two bullets, Brick leaned on a car near Rucker Park, right across the street from Polo Grounds. Holding the strap on the side of his leg to conceal it from view, he hawked an entry point into the projects. Bert was in the area, he got wind. In the neighborhood when receiving the intel, he rushed over.

The boy was the new leader of the Young Gunners, taking orders from Lady. This was all over the streets. Bert was not the average soldier; he got down and dirty like some of the best to come out of Polo Grounds. He was granted his current role because of this, *obviously*. But it didn't matter to Brick how *live* he was. In his eyes, the boy was only a baby, who deserved no accolades.

At one point, he could walk in-and-out of Polo Grounds without a hassle. Afterall, he was a DuPont, the family ruled over the projects. Now, however, he was banned from the sacred land of the DuPont's, *Polo Grounds*. If he showed his face there, it probably would be blown off. The Young Gunners wouldn't let him survive a few seconds. Therefore, his next move had to be with caution.

Pulling a hat low on his face, he proceeded across the street. One thing about himself, he was ready to die for what he believed in. That's what he was taught as a DuPont. *Go out blasting if you had to.* Thus, if he didn't make it out of Polo Grounds today, then so be it.

Entering the entry point he'd been scoping, just as his intel revealed, he noticed Bert right away.

Slipping.

Talking to a woman near a building, Bert leaned on a fence with his back to Brick, unaware of the emergence of his reaper. The woman faced Brick, giving him a sly wink as he approached.

No one else was outside.

Just the two.

As far as Brick could see.

Perfect.

This had to be one of his easiest kills. Bert really didn't know who he was playing with. Neither did Lady. Right now, in the palm of his hands, he had her top shooter, probably the only lifeline she had left in Harlem who would fight her battles. With Bert out the way, she would have a hell-of-a-time trying to fight off her enemies.

Moving slowly in Bert's direction, he elevated his weapon. About a few feet away from the boy, he walked on something that crunched beneath his feet.

Bert heard something to his rear and quickly turned around.

Oh shit!

It was Brick. His eyes moved to the man's hand. He had a gun.

A big one!

Quickly reaching for his strap, a flash from Brick's direction spun his body around, throwing him to the ground. The woman he was with was no longer present. Probably she ran off when realizing what was going on. Or had she set him up? Either way, he was in excruciating pain, suffering from a gunshot wound to the body.

Brick got over Bert, aiming his gun at the boy's face.

Bang!

There was no time to play around. After the first shot, he fired two more in Bert's chest before running off.

He made it to his car in one piece, parked across the street from the projects. Racing off the scene, he got to the eastside in no time.

In his apartment, he stashed his gun, changed clothes, and went right back outside.

Snap and a couple 'Mob members were out on the block.

"You always leave me out," voiced Snap.

"I don't know what you're talking about."

Brick had not told anyone he was going to get Bert. Only the woman who set the boy up knew his intentions. He knew her from Polo Grounds, had sexual relations with her in the past, and kept a deep connection. She was his eyes and ears on that side of town. Paying her a sum of cash, she helped set up Bert.

"Come on, big dog, I already got word about Polo Grounds."

Giving Snap a mean stare down, he watched the boys newly burned face like an eagle on the verge of swooping down on prey. He didn't like to be questioned, and most of his soldiers knew this. *Except Snap, I guess.*

His arm shot out, getting a death grip on Snap's neck.

The others present backed away, not wanting any parts of Brick's fury.

"You don't know not to question me?" Brick asked, taking out his gun, placing it beneath Snap's chin.

Frightened, Snap stared at Brick wide-eyed. His short life flashed before his eyes. He was almost positive Brick was on the verge of killing him.

It took everything in Brick's power not to kill Snap. His trigger-finger rattled in hesitancy as he held the gun to the boy. Oh, how he wanted to just pull the trigger.

But not now.

He released his grip on Snap.

He said, "Don't you ever question me," before walking off to his building.

Now was time to lay down his claim to take over the family. He'd accomplished the feat of taking out the boss of the Young Gunners, Bert. Before the crew got the chance to recoup, and find another leader, Brick had to follow up with some more mayhem. This was the plan. He was on it.

Chapter 20

Another death in the camp.

Damn, it!

How many more would there be?

"This shit is getting out of hand," Lady said to Drac on a jail call.

"Been outta hand. But that's just the streets. And what I've realized while in here, is there's no rules in the streets. A nigga really has no wins."

Drac sounded defeated.

Lady could hear it in his tone. In a way, she felt at fault for his current state of mind. Had she been sending the troops out more often, probably they would still have a foot on the competition's neck. But that was not the case. The opposition had scored a huge goal when they took out Bert, the last trustworthy Young Gunner leader.

"I heard, *you know who*, took out the young boy, b," said Drac. "How the fuck shorty let that nigga get up on him like that?"

"We can't really worry about that now, babe. The focus is on getting your mother outta those projects."

Word on the streets was that Bert was set-up by a woman in Polo Grounds and killed by Brick. The woman, Daphne, was killed right after by Young Gunner members for what she'd done. *Rightfully, so.*

"You're right. That nigga tried after my mom already; he'll definitely try his luck again."

"I spoke to her earlier. She doesn't seem like she wants to move, though."

"She's gonna have to. Unless she wants to die. Because after what happened to his mother, I doubt he gives two fucks whether she lives or dies."

"You're right about that. It's up to you now to try and convince her."

"I'm a get right on it."

Once through with the phone call with Drac, Lady prepared herself for some exercise, something she decided, of late, to get into. There was a gym on the complex that she was determined to utilize until it was time to head back home.

Dressing in some tights, a tank-top, she put on a pair of running-sneakers and shot out to the gym.

Spacious, the gym was surely something to talk about. Rock music played from a surround sound-system; different programs were being shown on various television sets situated throughout the gym. People worked out on treadmills, bicycles, and other machines. Some lifted weights.

Lady pondered what she should do. *Hmm...*

Catching sight of an elliptical machine, she was sold.

I'm a work on that.

Getting on the elliptical machine, she gripped its handles and began to step. Up-and-down. Up-and-down. Going at it for close to twenty-minutes, she paused, abruptly, when noticing a man enter the gym.

That can't be?

Thinking fast, she turned away so that she would not be noticed, but it was too late. The man had already saw her.

He was headed her way.

Hopping off the machine, she maintained a firm posture, holding her head high.

I'm not backing down from no smoke, b.

Though this had to be some sort of strange coincidence, or probably a set-up, she waited to see the outcome. Only if she'd carried a gun. Without hesitation, she would have shot the man. *Right in the gym.*

"Am I seeing right?" Mark asked, approaching Lady.

What were the odds of the current scene. Lady was beyond confused. *Perplexed.* Balling up her fists, she prepared for a throw-down.

She said, "Yeah, you seeing right, b. What's up?"

Mark tossed a blow in Lady's direction, missing a connection with her face by a few inches.

She saw the blow coming her way and quickly moved to the side, feeling the wind as it swooshed by. There was no way she could fight Mark. *He too big.* So she chose flight over fight. Taking off across the gym, Mark gave chase.

Everyone's attention was on the two.

An alarm went off, causing Mark to stop in his tracks. Looking around the gym, he figured he had better get out of dodge before the police was alerted.

Lady stopped running, pausing near a weight pile. She watched as Mark took flight out the gym as if someone were chasing him. *What's his problem?* But then she remembered. *He's on the run in New York.*

Unable to control his anger, he may have got himself in some shit.

"Are you okay?" someone asked her.

"Yeah. I'm cool."

Deciding to leave the gym, also, she went back to the house.

What the fuck just happened?

Did she just run into Mark?

What the fuck is the odds of that?

So many questions clouded her mind. There was no way possible Mark should have known where she was at. How did he know where she was at? Her mind only settled upon one person.

Ms. Elma.

Picking up a phone, she called the woman.

"You set me up, bitch!" she barked.

"What do you mean, Lady? I'm confused," responded Ms. Elma in a shocked voice.

"You let Mark know where I'm at! Don't think I'm fucking stupid, bitch!"

"Calm down, Lady. I would never do something like that. We are friends."

Shaking uncontrollably, she hung up on the woman.

She had to get out of the house. *Asap!*

Gathering her things, she called a taxi. She did not know where to go but knew she had better get out of Ms. Elma's house. Pacing the living room, she pondered the next move.

A knock came at the door.

Pausing, her heart raced. Beyond nervous, she tip-toed to the front-door to see who it was. Slowly, as quiet as possible, looking through a peephole, she saw that it was Paul. *What is he doing here?* She wasn't expecting the man. There was no reason for him to be here now.

This was *definitely* a set-up.

He knocked again. This time louder.

Lady continued to watch through the peephole.

Then he rang the doorbell.

Lady ignored the chime sound.

A phone rang in the background.

She ignored the phone and continued to watch Paul. *What's he up to?*

After a few more seconds, Paul walked off, leaving the premises.

Rushing to the phone, Lady picked up to call someone but realized someone was already on the phone. *Ms. Elma.*

"Lady, I don't know what's going on, but please give me a few seconds of your time," started Ms. Elma quickly.

Lady decided to hear her out.

She said, "Talk."

"I've never had any affiliation with Mark, never met him, *do not know him.* So how can I tell him where you're at?"

For some peculiar reason, Ms. Elma sounded sincere. Lady let her speak more.

"I will never set you up. That's not in my blood to do something like that. I look at you as a friend, not just a client. From the day I met you, I knew you were different."

"So why you sent Paul over here?" Lady asked. "And how did he get here so fast? What, you had him waiting around just in case Mark didn't get to me?" she said in a sarcastic tone.

"As I said, I will never set you up. When I spoke with you, and you blacked out on me, telling me that I let Mark know where you were, I figured something was wrong and called Paul. He just so happened to be in the neighborhood and said he would stop by. Did he get there yet?"

"He was at the door, but I didn't let him in."

"Paul knows a lot of people over there, so if there's a problem, he can help."

Lady felt more at ease now that Ms. Elma explained herself. However, she would still move with cautious. She was not in the clear yet.

"Well, tell him to get as much people together as possible. Mark is here, on the complex."

"Are you sure? It's kind of impossible to be let in that community."

"I'm positive. He swung at me in the gym."

"*He did what?*"

"Yep. He tried attacking me."

"Listen, I'm going to call Paul, again. I'm also going to call some people I know there on complex to find out what's really going on."

"Do what you gotta do. But have Paul bring me a gun when he comes back."

"I'll do that."

A knock came at the door minutes after Lady hung up with Ms. Elma. Investigating who was the knocker, she saw it was Paul. This time she let him in.

"Ms. Elma told me about everything. Are you okay?" Paul asked, holding a gun on his waist.

The manner in which Paul held his weapon showed that he was seasoned, possibly in the streets. His eyes searched the room as if he was looking for something out of place he could shoot.

"I'm cool," Lady said, now far more comfortable.

"You have your bags packed. I'm going to move you to another one of the houses."

"Yes."

"Let's go."

Outside four men awaited Paul. Two standing near a car. Two sitting inside the car. All were of Mexican descent. All were visibly strapped. The two inside the car had shotguns resting on the window ledges, while the other two held handguns, displayed.

"These are my guys," said Paul, ushering Lady into another car that he would be driving.

Inside the car, Lady was hurried out the complex, brought to another huge house in Hollywood Hills.

"This is my place," said Paul, letting her inside. "You'll be safe here."

"You sure?"

"Absolutely."

A phone rang in the spacious house.

Paul answered.

"Yes. She's here. Safe." Paul looked over at Lady and mouthed, *it's Ms. Elma.* "You got an ID on the guy? Okay, I'm on it."

He hung up.

"The guy is staying at the home of a huge drug baron. Her name is Jackie, and she's very heavy in the streets. Everything was caught on camera. He only came to the complex yesterday. So it's not like he knew you were there. It just so happened that you two ran into each other."

What is he doing in LA?

"I'll pay anything to get rid of him. Can one of your guys do the job?"

She hoped Paul bit the bullet. It would be a deed to Drac, *and herself*, if Mark was killed.

Looking straight in her eyes, Paul seemed as if he were searching for something. It was a few seconds before he responded, "Are you sure about that?"

Lady answered right away, "One hundred percent."

"Maybe I can help you."

"I'll pay anything."

Chapter 21

Relocating to the Marriot downtown LA, Mark was still in disbelief that he ran into Lady. *What the fuck is she doing out here?* Seeing the girl the day in the gym, his mind went blank. That Bronx mentality invaded his membrane, causing him to react in a manner he knew was not right. Lashing out at the girl, he missed her face by the skin of his teeth. Had the blow connected, she would have been out for the count. *For sure!* There was no doubt in his mind. He would have then stomped on her head, killing her right there. With his bare hands. There was, also, no doubt in his mind about that.

Sitting in his room, he cracked his knuckles.

Damn, that bitch got away.

He'd never been so close to Lady and was furious he missed the opportunity to pulverize her. *Break her into pieces.* If the scenario could play out once again, there were so many things he would have done different, he thought to himself. Over-and-over.

Staying at Jackie's pad was out of the question after the altercation. He left immediately following the incident. Phoning Jackie, she told him it would be best if he left as soon as possible. The elite who lived in the complex would not tolerate such an incident. They would surely call the police. Grabbing his things, he left. Jackie picked him up and carried him to the Marriot.

He made up his mind.

I'm going back to New York.

Calling Jackie, she answered on the first ring.

"You think you can get me on a private jet back to New York?" he said.

"Absolutely. You're leaving so soon?"

"Yeah. Too much drama on these sides. I can't take it anymore."

"Ah, man. Stop being a pussy."

Mark's mouth opened to say something, but he paused. This was one of the reasons, also, why he separated from Jackie. *Her potty-mouth.* There was one thing he learned coming up in the Bronx, *don't let a motherfucker talk to you certain ways.* And dealing with Jackie, one had to except her, at times, nasty ways.

He needed her assistance at the moment, so he would let her *mouth* slide for the time being.

"Can you get me on a flight today?" he said, ignoring her remark.

"Sure. But I think you should stay a little longer. I have another place you can stay at."

"Nah. I'm cool."

"Okay. Have it your way. Anyhow, who's that girl you had the altercation with?"

"This bitch from New York."

"Isn't she a DuPont, though?"

How this bitch know that? I never told her that?

"Where you get that info from?" he asked.

"I have sources."

It was true. Jackie had plenty of sources, informants that told her everything. So Mark saw no reason to worry about Jackie, he just wanted to get out of dodge and back to New York.

"Anyway. Please get me a flight."

"Be ready in the next couple of hours."

"Cool."

Mark couldn't wait to get back home. Regardless of what awaited him there. He preferred to battle it out there than in LA.

As he waited to depart Los Angeles, his father came to mind. *The Big Bull.* Things had really taken a turn for the worst. Never in a million years did he believe he would be the one to kill his own father.

Bill.

His brother, also.

Tears began to pour from his eyes, as they always did when he was alone with his thoughts. For what occurred, he was sure to blame. Attempting to take over the family was sure to cause problems, he knew. There was no way Big Bear, or his sons were just going to sit around and watch this occur. Nor his own father. It just was not how the DuPont structure was. And would never be. The clan was ruled by Big Bear, *that's it!* And would always be, no matter who tried to take over.

"I fucked up, man."

Mark sobbed aloud, unable to control his emotions. He was hurt. The pain inside was unbearable. He'd done wrong by his family.

Crying himself to sleep, he got up when a call came in from Jackie.

"A pickup guy is downstairs. He'll bring you where you need to go."

"A pickup guy?" Mark asked. "What you mean? We didn't discuss nobody coming to pick me up. I thought you would pick me up."

"Listen, Mark, you've made it clear a thousand times you didn't want to be with me. I shouldn't even be helping your ass out. But I still do have some love for you, that's my *only* reason being of assistance to you.

I'm with my man right now and can't come to get you. I sent over one of my guys. He'll bring you to the clear port, where there's a jet waiting. All courtesy of *me*."

Mark did not like Jackie's tone. It took everything in his power to not tell her to *suck a dick*. He would just wait until he got back to New York to call and tell her his true feelings.

"Aight. I'm going down now."

"Call me when you get across."

Jackie hung up.

"Fucking bitch," fumed Mark, grabbing a bag and heading out the door.

Down in the hotel lobby, a tall, black man waited on him.

"Mark?" he questioned as soon as Mark exited the hotel's elevator.

"Yeah. That's me."

The man stretched out his hand for a shake.

Mark shook the man's hand and walked toward the hotel's exit. He was ready to just be gone out of California.

A black Suburban waited outside.

The tall, black man signaled that the truck was their ride.

Mark got inside, relaxing in the back seat.

The man got in the driver's seat and drove off.

As the vehicle maneuvered toward its destination, Mark, his head resting back in the seat, looked out at the sunny California sky. Thinking about what he would do when he reached New York. Money would not be a problem. *Never had.* So he didn't have to go back to the hustle and rob game. He could just find a nice apartment somewhere in the cut, away from everything, and just chill.

Yeah, I'm a do that.

Rolling down the window to take in some breeze, he rested his head back and shut his eyes. The pressure of late was unbearable, but he fought through the storm, regardless. It was difficult to cope with certain losses life had tossed his way for sure. Being from the slums of the Bronx, though, had taught him to stand firm through anything. And that's what he'd do. Nothing could break him. He would not allow it.

The car rolled to a stop, and he opened his eyes to get a glimpse at where they'd reached. A pistol was pointed at his face, held by what seemed to be a Mexican. Scoping the environment, he realized he was in a back street somewhere. *How the fuck I get here?* He'd only closed his eyes for a few minutes.

Regardless, he was now staring down the barrel of a pistol.

A big one!

Jackie had set him up. There was no doubt in his mind about that. *Why,* though? Yes, they've had multiple issues in the past, *relationship wise*, but none to the level where he felt she wanted him dead. Obviously, that was not the case, though. The pistol pointed at his face proved the contrary of what he thought.

The driver kept his head straight as if he did not know what was going on in the back. Had Mark not opened the window, the shooter would not have had such a clear shot if he decided to shoot. By the look of the Mexican's eyes, a young man, he looked like he was on the verge of squeezing the trigger. So Mark closed his eyes, tightly, hoping this would somehow ease the pain when his face was shot.

Boom!

Chapter 22

The Mob dismantled the stronghold of the Young Gunners in Polo Grounds, running the latter out the projects. *Completely.* Those that stuck around submitted to the takeover, joining forces with the victor in the battle. They had no choice. It was either that or vacate the premises.

Perched in the center of Polo Grounds, Brick was surround by The Mob, taking in the view of his new playground. Though the projects had always been ruled by DuPont's, it was a new day. A DuPont, other than Big Bear's offspring, finally made it to the top.

"You checked the apartment to see if she's still there?" Brick asked Snap.

"Hell yeah. We broke down the door, searched the whole apartment." Snap shook his head. "No sign of her. She gone."

One of the biggest staples in Polo Grounds was gone. Cheryl had vacated the scene with everyone else. *She better had.* Had this not been the case, Brick would have surely ended her life. There was no way she could stick around while he held the reign as king.

Fuck no!

He said, "That's good."

It was surreal to be an eastside Harlem kid that ended up ruling over the craziest projects on the westside. The only person, in the history of the neighborhood, who had accomplished such a feat was Big Bear, when he went on the eastside, *as a westside nigga,* and took over some significant turfs. He had to admit, Big Bear was a bad motherfucker!

But Brick's aspirations didn't stop in Polo Grounds. He wanted the entire westside of Harlem under the The Mob's rule.

"Let's make a step. I wanna go and see my Jamaican friends."

Building a pact with the Jamaicans made Brick's empire stronger. The foreigners, who were wild cowboys, were a significant force to have on the team. Their affiliation was surely necessary.

The Mob members rolled up and headed over to 145th and Edgecombe Avenue.

It was a damp day. The sky was cloudy, seeming on the verge of exploding into rain. Besides a few passerby's no one was out on 145th, more than likely fearing to get caught in the sure advent of rain.

It was about ten 'Mob members with Brick, crowding the block. Five went off to stand on one side of the street. Five played the side Brick was on. This was how the gang usually moved. *Strategically.* Just in case something kicked off.

"I'm a go check this nigga in the building," said Brick. "Watch the street." He gestured with his head. "Snap, let's role."

Entering a building, inside was empty of occupants. The usual noise of activity inside apartments blared out into the halls. Loud television sets; people talking; arguing; music playing; children screaming at the top of their lungs; among other things.

Brick made way to an apartment on the first floor, knocking the door.

Donovan opened after audibly looking through a peephole.

"What's going on?" he asked, stepping out in the halls to speak with Brick.

Brick could hear children in the background of Donovan's apartment; a Jamaican lady shouted at them about their behavior.

"It's dead outside, man. What happened to your guys?" Brick asked.

"It's a day party out in the Bronx today so they went over the bridge."

"So why you didn't go?"

"My kids just came up from Jamaica. I'm gearing up to bring them down to Florida." Donovan shook his head. "Can't have them around this crazy New York."

"I was just passing through to let you know that I appreciate your assistance in the battle." Brick smiled. "We won."

Donovan kept a serious face, shaking his head. His eyes roamed from Brick to Snap every few seconds.

Why did he bring that youth?

Snap avoided Donovan's side-eyes, keeping his focus mainly on Brick.

"But check it. It's time to broaden The Mob's reach," said Brick.

"What you mean?" Donovan wanted to know. Confused.

"I don't know why you would be out here alone."

Brick's arm shot to Donovan's throat, grabbing a hold of the man's neck.

Snap went into action, following his bosses lead, even though he had no idea Brick would react in the manner he had. Taking out his gun, without asking questions, he aimed at Donovan's head.

Struggling to break free of Brick's grasp, Donovan ducked just as Snap fired a shot at his cranium.

Boom!

Pain shot through Brick's arm when Snap's shot missed Donovan, hitting him instead in the hand. The pain was unbearable. Grabbing his hand where he was shot, he hopped away toward the building's exit.

While Brick sauntered off toward the building's exit, Snap kept an eye on Donovan, who was trying to escape inside his apartment.

Boom! Boom! Boom!

Firing three more rounds, all of which connected with Donovan's back, he moved toward the man, who'd fallen right inside his apartment.

The woman and children screamed in the background, loud enough to wake a sleeping neighbor.

Snap didn't care, though. He knew what Brick expected of him, so he did the dirt he was recruited in The Mob to do.

Donovan, on the floor, was in excruciating pain, suffering from three bullets to the back. How had he allowed Brick to get up so close? He should have known better.

Taking aim at Donovan's face, Snap fired a round, which slammed through the man's forehead, shooting through the floor beneath his body.

Donovan's body jerked once before going completely still.

Aiming the gun in the apartment, Snap let off a succession of rounds before running outside.

"Get in the fucking car!" shouted Brick from the passenger seat of a ride driven by one of his henchmen, waiting outside for Snap.

Snap ran to the car and got inside.

"You shot me, motherfucker," Brick said.

His arm was wrapped in a white towel that was stained with blood.

"I'm sorry, man. But I killed that nigga."

"You got him for sure?"

"For sure. He's dead to the world."

The news of Donovan's demise made Brick proud. He'd done what his family couldn't, *kill Donovan*.

His initial intentions were not to kill the man. Though it was a plan for the future, he never expected it to happen so fast. Of course, Donovan had to go; he spilled DuPont blood. But he was playing things by the air, waiting for the perfect moment to take out the Jamaican gangster. It just so happened that the perfect moment presented itself, *sooner than later*. When he noticed none of Donovan's goons were around, that the man was completely by himself, his thoughts went into action. Grabbing the man, he went to reach for his gun to shoot, but Snap beat him to the punch, shooting him instead. Regardless of how it played out, Donovan was no longer among the land of the living.

"I gotta get to a hospital. But I can't go nowhere in Harlem. Police gonna be checking spots out here for shooting victims," he said. "Get to a spot in Queens or something."

Brought to Jamaica Hospital in Queens, Brick walked himself in through a crowded waiting area to a front desk.

"I was shot," he said to two female nurses.

He raised his arm so they could see. By now the towel was completely soaked with his blood. And he didn't know if he were hallucinating or not, but he felt somewhat weak.

"Oh my," voiced one of the women. "He looks like he's leaking."

Both women got up and came around the desk. They ushered Brick into a back room where doctors, right away, began to tend to his wound.

Chapter 23

"I really like it out here. I always have."

Cheryl expressed her sentiments about being in Los Angeles.

"Me, too. That's why I decided to make it home."

Cruising through Santa Monica in California, Lady felt, somewhat, at peace. It was like she was floating on clouds. So much had changed in her life that she was grateful for. Losses surely rocked her world when they came. But the wins outweighed the losses. *For sure.*

Purchasing multiple properties in Los Angeles, her eyes were now set on San Diego, a section of the state she loved. More-and-more, she became infatuated with the real estate game, building her own empire, which had gotten on the way. Life was surely bestowing some blessings on her. Never in the world she would have imagined to be in her current position as a leading woman.

"I should have been left those nasty projects. It cost my boy his life." Cheryl shook her head in shame. "Had I just broken out of that comfort zone and embrace the blessings God placed in my way, many things would not have happened to me."

"One thing I've learned in life, is that we can't beat up ourselves about past mistakes. We just have to fight to not make the same ones."

Cheryl shook her head.

"That's true."

"Losing my mother made me realize so many things."

"You know," started Cheryl, pausing, looking off outside for a few seconds, "I knew your mother. She and 'Bear had a thing going on."

Taken aback by Cheryl's bold statement, Lady did not know what to say. She had no idea Cheryl was aware of her mother's relationship with her husband.

"It's okay," said Cheryl, "you were only a little girl. 'Bear had many mistresses. In and outside the projects. He was a playboy in his day. Probably still is." She smiled.

Lady kept quiet.

"But that's my Big Bear," Cheryl continued. "He gave me two beautiful boys." Her voiced cracked. As usual, when she spoke about her boys, she got emotional, especially when thinking about Kevin.

Lady continued to keep quiet, allowing Cheryl to vent. It had to be hard to lose two sons, one to the streets, the other, possibly, to prison. She didn't know what she would do if ever confronted with such an issue. Cheryl was a strong woman, and she commended her on that.

A tear fell from Cheryl's eye. She quickly wiped it away.

"I'm sorry. I just get over emotional about things."

"Let it out, Cheryl. It's all good. You're a strong woman, and as long as I'm around, I got your back," Lady stated with surety.

"I appreciate that."

Cheryl had to vacate Polo Grounds. Brick's move on the projects threatened her well-being. To make matters worse, he voiced his intentions on what he would do if he caught her in his grasp.

Deep down, Cheryl respected Brick's stance. What Big Bear had done to his mother was wrong. He had every right to react how he was. Cheryl would have done the same thing. So she had nothing against Brick. Currently, he was in power, and his position had to be respected. Leaving Polo Grounds was necessary to the order of the day.

Lady didn't have to speak with Drac to know what she had to do. Once learning that Cheryl was in danger, she situated for her to come to California.

Cheryl hopped on a plane and came without hesitation.

With the help of Paul, Lady was able to have Mark murdered. His body was found in an alley somewhere in

Compton with a bullet wound to the face. He'd finally met his maker. The news of his death brought Lady to tears. She knew, ultimately, he was responsible for her mother's murder. Whether directly or indirectly. His connection to the Jamaicans caused her mother's demise. She was so happy he was gone. And, to make matters even better, Donovan, the actual culprit behind her mother's murder, was killed in Harlem, along with one of his children.

Someone went to the man's apartment, called him outside, opened fire on him, and then shot up his apartment. Attempting to get clear of a volley of bullets rattling the apartment, a young boy was killed, which turned out to be Donovan's son.

Lady didn't like that a young boy was killed but smiled when hearing about Donovan's brutal killing. He deserved everything that came his way. She hoped he was rotting in hell.

"Things just got crazy…real fast," said Cheryl, shaking her head. "I've never seen anything like this before in the family. Everyone pretty much knew their place. But I guess the *young* wanted a chance at being on top."

"I totally agree with that."

Cheryl was right. The younger generation wanted a shot at carrying the torch, and now they finally got the chance.

"But regardless of how they feel, it's impossible for them to carry the torch. *Fully that is*. Big Bear set things up to where only he and sons could rule, and no one else. From the properties to the businesses, the money, everything is owned by Big Bear and his offspring. No matter how anyone fought to control the family, they could probably have Polo Grounds, which is actually owned by the city, but everything else is in paperwork."

Cheryl had solidified what Lady had been thinking all along. *What was the fight to control the family for? A name?* Because, at the end of the day, that's the *only* thing one could gain. *A name.* The DuPont empire consisted of property, businesses, offshore accounts, among other things. All of which was in Big Bear's name. Thus, there was no real reason for the fighting. It was not like if someone got hold of the family from Big Bear that they would end up with all his assets. They would probably have a huge name in the streets, *but has that ever paid the bills?*

"I've always wondered about the reason for the fighting," said Lady.

"Ego." Cheryl shook her head. "It's all a bunch of ego."

Just as Lady thought.

Ego.

It was time to explore the terrain of California, get more familiar with her new home. Already, she had a few properties in the jungles of Los Angeles that she got for little to nothing. Daily, she visited communities as Compton, Watts, Inglewood, and other downtrodden neighborhoods to see what was on the market. *Eventually these areas will be gentrified*, Ms. Elma made note. So it was best, no matter how the neighborhoods looked, for Lady to get on board from now and get a piece of the pie.

Ms. Elma had not led her wrong so far, so Lady would continue to follow the woman's lead.

Afterward

It was a hot day in Harlem. The temperature was somewhat unbearable. Many stayed indoors under air conditioners to avoid the record-breaking New York weather.

Dressed in shorts, no shirt, Brick's buff physique caught the attention of everyone passing by. Doing pull-ups on W. 155th Street on a light pole, a few of his men stood close by, awaiting their turn to go.

Exercise was the order of the day among his troops. It was imperative that everyone stayed in shape, a thing he learned while in jail. In the streets, he followed this regimen. Religiously. Mostly everyday he worked out, sticking to, mainly, calisthenics. Pull-ups, push-ups, and dips was all he needed to keep his body hardened. He didn't need any weights.

Since taking over Polo Grounds, he moved into the projects, figuring this to be the best course of action to take. With his presence, resistors would think twice to rebel. There were surely a few persons around who were advocates of Big Bear's rule, though undercover, who were just waiting for him to slip up so that they could move in. But there was no way he would slip up.

No way.

"Get up there, Snap," he instructed after getting down.

Snap climbed up the pole, gripping the handles of the light device. Going up-and-down a few times, he got down.

"That's what I'm talking about." Brick boasted. "You gotta get this fucking money."

Getting in a few more sets, Brick decided to head to his new apartment in Polo Grounds. Cheryl's old pad. After she left in fear of her life, he changed the locks and took over the place. He felt right at home in the apartment.

Going in to freshen up, he came back out into the halls when he was done. A few of his men sat in the halls waiting on him. Going over to a window that looked below outside onto the court, he searched the scene.

"Dudes think that just because they was not a part of the DuPont's that they could just hustle freely in the projects."

Two boys were out in the courtyard committing hand-to-hand crack deals.

"They must not know who I am." Brick watched the boys.

His men came over to watch, also.

He ordered, "Snap, go and bring them niggas upstairs to me."

Snap shot downstairs following Brick's orders.

When Snap got outside, Brick watched the exchange between his soldier and the boys. The boys were resistant, as he figured they would be, until Snap pulled out a gun and ordered them inside the building.

They followed his command after that.

After a while, the elevator dinged and Snap exited with the boys, both of whom looked horrified.

Brick approached the duo.

"Who told y'all to hustle in my projects?"

"Listen, OG, I don't want no problems," spoke up one of the boys. "I always bust a couple sales every now and again. Never knew it was a problem."

Brick cracked a smile. He respected the boy's honesty.

"I respect that," he said, shaking his head. "You're a real one."

Snap and the rest of 'Mob looked like they wanted to eat the boys. Their mouths seemingly drooled as they looked from the prey to their boss, waiting, *impatiently*, for him to give word of approval for them to slaughter the boys.

Taking out a Colt .45 from his waist, Brick admired the gun, twirling it in every which direction. He then put the nozzle to one of the boys' head, focusing in on the victim as he did so.

The boy was scared for his life. Looking at Brick, tears poured from his eyes. His friend, next to him, also began to cry.

Brick said, "Real men don't cry. Tears won't help a sure trip to the cemetery."

"But why are you doing this?" the boy asked.

"Because I have to set an example, so a next nigga won't make the same mistake."

Brick pulled the trigger.

A bullet escaped the weapon's chamber, slamming through the boy's forehead before exiting through the back with a splash of brain matter that decorated a close by wall. Instantly, the boy fell backwards, his body, headfirst, slamming into a wall.

Following Brick's lead, Snap shot the next boy, who tried escaping. Holding him by the shirt collar, he pumped multiple bullets into the boy's frame.

…to be continued.

Also by Nadir

Down for Her Brooklyn Thug
Down for Her Brooklyn Thug 2
Bucktown Hittaz
She a Thug and He a Square
Boyz in Blue
Boyz in Blue 2
Boyz in Blue 3
Gunsmoke
The Thugtress of Harlem